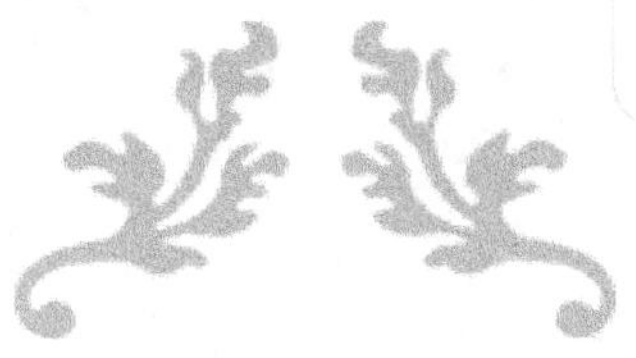

St. Lucia Escapades

St. Lucia Escapades

Michelle Kee

Published by Michelle Kee, 2023.

This is a work of fiction. Similarities to real people, places, or events are entirely coincidental.

ST. LUCIA ESCAPADES

First edition. September 14, 2023.

Copyright © 2023 Michelle Kee.

Written by Michelle Kee.

Copyright © 2020 Michelle Kee

All rights reserved. This is a work of pure fiction. Names, characters and incidents are pure products of the author's mind and not reality. Any resemblance to actual events, people or places are strictly coincidental.

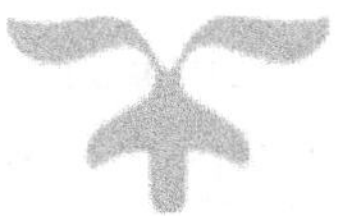

CHAPTER ONE

Moira

The End. Leaning back in her desk chair and smiling, Moria Donovan let out a relieved sigh. Finally, the rough draft for her latest novel was finished. This book had given her fits from the beginning. Even though she had plotted the story out, the second she began typing, the story took on a life of its own. That can be both a good thing and a pain in the ass for an author. Leaning forward, she moved the mouse. She quickly compiled the files, saved them and shot them off to her editor in New York. Once the email was sent, she shut down her computer, picked up her empty coffee cup and stood from the desk.

Moira headed for her kitchen, rolling her shoulders as she moved. She had awakened at around five that morning and unable to fall back asleep decided to try and get some writing done. It had worked too. Reaching her red Mr. Coffee pot, she refilled her coffee. Glancing at her moving cat clock, you know the ones, the ones where the eyes and tail move, before taking her cell from the charging dock on the counter. Exiting the room and heading for her back deck, she dialed her mom.

"Hello,"

"Mornin' Ma." Moria greeted, her Irish blood playing out in her voice.

"Oh, Moira my baby. I'm surprised yer' callin'. Your Da and I figured you'd be locked in yer' office writing." Maureen Donovan chuckled, her own Irish lilt that matched Moira's relaxed Moira even more.

"I had a bout of inspiration this mornin' and was able to finish. I sent it to Holly about five minutes ago."

Moira dropped into one of her deck chairs and breathed in the fresh spring morning. She loved DC in the spring. Especially in the area where her ground floor apartment was. Three blocks to the east was a park that was bursting with flowers this time of year. Not mention her neighbors on either side had hanging flowerpots on the decks. So yeah, the smell of flowers was everywhere around her right now and she loved it.

"That's wonderful me darlin'. I can't wait to read it. When were you hoping to release it again?"

"Well, now the release date is set for September seventeenth. It will be at least two, maybe three weeks before Holly will get the rough draft back to me."

"It's April now, so barring any setbacks, this one will be ready by what, end of June?"

Moira laughed, "Aye Ma. You sound like Holly."

Maureen snorted on the other end, *"Considering you've been doing this since yer last year of college, yer ol' Ma has picked up a few things."*

"Yer not old Ma."

"Bless you dear, but I feel it sometimes."

Moira took a sip of her coffee, "I hear you and Da are planning to retire at the end of the year."

"Aye, we are. Yer Da is sixty-four and so am I for that matter. It's time. I've been a nurse for forty-two years and your Da a Garda for just as long. We're too old for this."

Garda, Irish slang for police. Moira and her older brother Sean had been so proud of the life their parents had built for not only them, but for her and Sean as well. "And what will you two do with all that time? Travel?" Moira questioned.

"We've talked of that aye. Your Da would like to go back and visit Ireland again. We've no' been back since yer grandparents died. You and Sean were only wee bairns then. It would be nice to see Belfast now, without all the troubles that were there when yer Da and I were growing up."

"You and Da should. You two have always talked about going back to visit."

"Aye. Well, let us get through the end of the year first." Maureen laughed. *"Now, I believe the tradition when ye finish a book is that you, me, and your Da have dinner out."*

"Yes, and keepin' with tradition it's Da's turn to pick where." Moira grinned.

"That it is. He's at the station today, so I will call him and text you later this afternoon when he gets home."

"Sounds like a plan. I'm going to get a shower, then I think I'll go for a jog in the park. It's such a beautiful day."

"You be careful out there and enjoy your run. Is breá liom tú."

Moira couldn't help but smile hearing her mother say, 'I love you' in the native Irish, "Is breá liom tú, ró-mamaí."

"See, good thing me and your Da insisted you and Sean learn to speak Irish." Maureen teased.

Moira couldn't argue that. Hell, she had to admit, Irish was a very musical language and it kept that bond between her and Sean even stronger when they were young. They could talk to each other and not worry about being overheard since Irish wasn't a language you heard much in America, even in DC. It was like their own private club. Moira said bye to her mom, polished off her coffee then headed inside to change for her jog.

***

Cord

"Well, damnit all to hell." Cord O'Brien grumbled lowly as he stood in the empty room surveying the damage before him.

"It's not as bad as it looks actually," his brother Collen began. "The second the sprinklers started the fire department was in route."

"But there was still enough damage to cause us to shut this place down for what, three maybe four weeks?" Cord pointed out.

"Three." Collen sighed.

Cord gnashed his teeth and kicked at an empty beer bottle that had been dropped. Last night, some drunk college frat boy decided to re-enact a scene from Coyote Ugly and in turn, damned near burnt the bar down. Luckily, this particular bar was two blocks away from a fire house, so the firemen got there in less than two minutes and even luckier still, no one had been hurt. Cord ran his hand through his dark mahogany brown hair in frustration.

"What do we know about the kid that started this?"

Collen cleared his throat, "The kid is a senior at NYU. The cops arrested him for drunk and disorderly, destruction of public property and public endangerment since the place was packed last night. The kid's father has already reached out and wants to meet with us this morning."

Cord growled, "No doubt to minimize the situation. Alright, call the dad and let's meet over at the diner. If I'm going to do this, I'm going to need food."

Half an hour later, seated at Cord's favorite New York diner, he and Collen watched in shock as the councilman for the Upper West side, Eugene Walker, walked in and joined them, "Good morning gentlemen."

"Um, morning Councilman Walker." Cord managed to say.

"Look, let's not beat around the bush. Because of last night's events the three of us have a lot on our plates this morning," as Walker started things off.

"What are you wanting Mr. Walker?" Collen questioned, expecting the councilman to offer money to make this go away.

"What I want? I want to use this as a teaching exercise for my son." At the O'Brien brothers' confused looks, Walker elaborated. "You see, my wife tends to spoil our son James. Last night was the tipping point for me. I'm going to teach that boy that his actions have consequences. What I'm offering gentlemen is simple. Not only will my son pay for the damages out of his trust fund, but he will also help in getting your place cleaned up and running."

Cord and Collen were floored. This city official was not only offering to pay, but he wasn't trying to buy them off to keep his son out of the papers. "You're serious sir? The press will no doubt..."

"It's Cord O'Brien, right?" Walker asked and Cord nodded. "Cord, as I've said, for too long James has believed he can do what he wants with no consequences. That stops now. After last night's little stunt, his mother has finally agreed that James needs to be taught a lesson."

"And the press? We doubt we could keep the identity of your son out of this for too long." Collen added.

"I'll handle the press. I'm not going to minimize this and will be telling the truth. And before you ask, no this is not some PR spin to win votes. I may be a New York councilman, but I'm first and foremost a father." Walker said. "So, do we have a deal gentlemen?"

Cord and Collen looked at each other then back at Walker. Cord spoke then, "Councilman Walker, you have a deal."

***

Moira

Moira sat with her parents at their favorite Italian restaurant near the National Mall. Kiernan Donovan lifted his wine glass in toast to his daughter, "To Moira, on the completion of yet another novel. Sláinte."

"Sláinte." Moira and her mom repeated.

"What will you do now?" Maureen asked.

"I haven't really thought of that yet." Moira admitted.

"Perhaps, this will help." Kiernan smiled handing her an envelope.

Knitting her brows, Moira accepted it and slowly opened it. What she saw inside had her gasping. It was airline tickets and a reservation for a private beach condo in St. Lucia. She knew her jaw had to have hit the floor and her eyes wide when she looked up at her parents. "Ma, Da, this is...this is too..."

"No, m'iníon." Kiernan interrupted, "Yer Ma and I, along with Sean have been planning this for some time now. After yer Ma told me, I called Sean and he agreed that now was perfect."

Moira got a little teary-eyed. Especially when her father had said *'M'iníon', "my daughter"* in Irish. "I...I donna know what to say."

Maureen reached over and took her daughter's hand, "You can say thank you and have a good time."

Moira felt laughter bubble up as she pushed out of her chair. She moved to her parents and hugged them both. Moira thanked God every day that she was blessed with such a loving and accepting family. When she had told them, she wanted to be a writer when she was in high school, her parents had simply told her to follow her passion. The same could be said when Sean wanted to join the Marines after 9/11. Not once did her parents set limits on her or Sean.

"It was Laura that picked the condo. She teased Seany that he didna' understand your tastes." Maureen added.

"Thank God. I love me brother, but in this case, Laura is right. I'll call them both tonight and thank them." Moira smiled, tucking the envelope into her purse.

***

Moira sat on her back deck watching the full moon rise over the city of her birth, sipping her wine. After dinner with her parents, she had called Sean and his wife Laura and thanked them. Sean had told her that she worked too hard and after ten years as an author she deserved a vacation. She couldn't argue with him. She had published her first novel her senior year of college and from there, her career had flourished. It was about three years later she had met her ex. While their relationship had seemed to be idyllic, she quickly discovered his true colors. Moira chastised herself for thinking about that time in her life. Tonight, was a night for celebrating.

In a week, she would be boarding a plane and going to the beautiful St. Lucia for three weeks. She had only seen pictures of the islands and what she had seen looked like paradise. She had only met one person who had ever been there and that had been her assistant editor of the college newspaper Roxanne. Roxi had told Moira that if she ever got to go, she would fall in love with the islands. Moira would call her in the morning and get some ideas for places to visit. Roxi would know places not on the beaten path and that's what Moira wanted.

Polishing off the sweet read, Moira pushed herself up from the lounger she was in and headed inside. Even though her book was in the hands of her editor, she still had a bit of work to do before she left. Most people had no idea the time and energy that went into being an author. It wasn't just writing. Despite having a publishing house backing her, Moira still had to do her share of the work on marketing and promotion. These she did through her website and social media, but she also reached out to public publications like The Voice in New York and several others like it. Placing her empty glass in the sink, Moira started clicking off her lights as she headed for bed.

CHAPTER TWO

Cord

He couldn't believe that he had let his brother and parents talk him into this. Renovations were starting on the bar and damnit he should be there to oversee things. Instead, where was he? A beautiful beach condo on the shore of St. Lucia. A place he had not visited in nearly twenty years, but hey, who was counting. He stepped out onto his deck as his mind replayed how he had wound up here in paradise.

That morning when he had shown up at the bar that Councilman Walker's son nearly burned down, he had been stopped by not just his brother Collen, but by the bar's manager Taylor, and the head bartender Angie. Before he could speak, the three had proceeded to tell him that as of that moment he was on vacation for three weeks. When he tried to argue, Collen stopped him. Collen, who knew the business of their seven bars better than even Cord at times, reminded him of that.

"Cord, I know these bars are your babies, hell their mine too. And have you forgotten that I've been involved with you in this venture since damned near the beginning back in college?"

"No, I haven't forgotten Collen."

"Then, as not just your business partner but your brother, I'm telling you that I've got this. Go on vacation. It's been what...three, four years since you've taken any real time away?" Collen inquired.

Cord had sighed then and rubbed the back of his neck, "Yeah, I guess you're right."

"Of course, I'm right. You're not the only one that got brains in this family." Collen had laughed.

Cord couldn't stop the smile as the ocean breeze washed over him. He had to admit, his little brother knew him better that Cord knew himself. He and Collen had worked so hard to build their business. What had started as one bar near the NYU campus had now expanded into seven bars throughout the five boroughs. That alone was beyond anything Cord and Collen had imagined when they began. Standing there watching the jewel like water before him ebb and flow, the sweet smell of the tropical flora that surrounded his villa along with the call of the birds had him more relaxed than he could remember. Hell, he was here in paradise and his family wanted him to enjoy himself. He decided then and there that he would do just that. He pulled his phone from his pocket and shot a quick text to his family:

Okay guys, you sent me here and now that I'm here...I'm glad you did. You all want me to relax and have fun so that's what I'm gonna do. Mom, pop, I'll call ya each night. Collie... unless there's a major problem, do not call me.

See ya in three weeks,

Cord

Hitting send, Cord turned and walked back inside. He jumped into the shower to wash off the travel from New York to St. Lucia. He dressed in his favorite pair of khaki shorts, a blue cotton polo style shirt and a pair of flip-flops. Before leaving the condo, he put on his faded Atlanta Braves ball cap and stepped out into the island paradise that was St. Lucia with a fresh spring in his step and a huge smile plastered on his handsome face.

***

Moira

The sky was clear and the water a beautiful azure blue. She couldn't remember if she had ever seen water as blue as the water, she was looking at right now. The second she had disembarked from her plane; excitement had filled her. When Roxi had found out she was going to St. Lucia, Roxi had immediately emailed Moira a list of places to see and things to do. Of course, being the club girl that Roxi was, she had made sure to list a few clubs that she figured Moira would like. Moira wasn't much of a club or bar goer, but she figured why not.

Once the Uber had dropped her off at the condo her parents, brother and sister-in-law had rented for her, she quickly unpacked and explored the condo. It was bright, airy, and so much light filtered through the numerous windows. She had opened the windows and let the sea air flow through the condo. Currently, she was standing at the railing of her deck looking over the majestic view of the Caribbean ocean before her. Already, her artistic mind was thinking of how she could use her experience here in a future novel.

Moira turned and hurried back inside and went straight to her purse and pulled out her traveling writer's notebook and a pen. Returning to the deck, she went straight to work jotting down what she was seeing, smelling, and feeling. This was something she had done ever since she was a sophomore in high school whenever she and her family would travel to a new place. She would write down thoughts, smells, feelings, and sights.

Ten minutes later, she had her purse slung across her chest and was walking in the direction of the town where she was. All around her tourists and locals moved along the streets. It was early, but already she could smell the delicious scents of food wafting in the air mixing with the flora and sea air. It imbued her with an energy she hadn't felt since her days in college when she, Roxi, and their other roommate Lucinda had gone to Key West for spring break. She loved it and would definitely do something as a thank you for her family for doing this for her.

Moira had spotted a little cafe to her right, and feeling hunger starting to gnaw at her, she walked in. She was quickly seated and began looking over her menu. The waiter came by and after taking her order and bringing her a glass of water, Moira sat back and just people watched. One of her favorite past times. Sometimes, in DC, she would go to The National Mall, or one of the many parks and just watch people. Tourists, families, politicians, lots of those in the Nation's Capital. Lifting her glass of water, she smiled and nodded when the waiter returned with a cup and carafe of coffee. Before she could lift her coffee cup, she spotted a man walking in and taking a seat at the bar.

He was tall, about six foot three, maybe four. He was handsome, probably one of, if not the most handsome man she had ever seen in person. He was dressed in khaki shorts, a blue shirt, flip-flops, and a ball cap. Sipping her coffee, she studied the man. He moved and talked with the person at the bar with a smoothness and confidence that said whoever he was, he was successful. She was guessing he was an American, but since she couldn't hear him, she couldn't be sure. After a few more minutes of watching him with a strange fascination, she was brought out of her study when her food arrived. Breathing in the smell of the food had her moaning quietly. Wasting no time, she picked up her fork and dug in.

***

Cord

Cord sipped his beer as he waited for his lunch. He didn't know if it was because he himself was a bar owner or what, but whenever he went to a restaurant that had a bar, he typically sat at the bar. He turned on the stool and cast a casual glance around the dining room. Tourists and locals sat at the tables and booths. Now, he was the only person at the bar, but in a few hours that would change he suspected. His hazel green eyes stopped at a lone woman thoroughly enjoying her lunch. She would stand out in just about any crowd. She was petite, from what he could tell with her sitting, she looked to be curvy in all the places he believed a woman should be. He wondered, if she stood, would she have that classic hourglass figure? Then there was her hair.

Rivers of flaming red gentle curls cascaded over her shoulders and down to the middle of her back. From his vantage point, it looked soft and silky despite the curls. What would it look like as the dawning sun caressed it against her pillow? Okay, where the hell had that thought come from? Cord frowned slightly. He liked women but the thoughts that seemed to be flowing through his mind watching this stranger was a new concept for him. He shook his head slightly before taking another sip of his beer. He had just turned back to face the bar again when his food was placed in front of him.

"Wow, this looks delicious." Cord grinned.

"It's a local favorite. Enjoy." The bartender replied, before leaving Cord to enjoy his meal.

As he ate, he covertly continued to study the woman. There was more to his interest than just her being beautiful. Hell, he lived in New York City for crying out loud and as the owner of seven popular bars, he came across beautiful women on a nightly basis. So, what was it about this red-haired beauty that captivated him? Cord was halfway through his meal when he saw her rise from the table, toss down a few bills, then head for the door.

'Damn, she is a looker. That hair, that body.' Cord thought as he felt his cock start to harden in his shorts.

***

Moira

Moira had spent the afternoon just wandering around the area. Taking in the vibrancy of the small island. The island truly was a Caribbean jewel. Already, she had a semi game plan for the next day. She was currently walking along the beach toward her condo to grab a quick nap. It was nearly three in the afternoon and the afternoon heat was at its peak. She sighed walking into the coolness of her condo, glad she remembered to close the windows and click on the AC units. Dropping her large straw bag and hat on the sofa, she pulled off her sandals before moving through the living area toward the bedroom. Stripping down to her bra and panties, Moira slipped beneath the cool sheets and felt herself drifting off.

About two hours later, Moira awakened. Sitting up, she stretched her arms over her head noticing the fading light as the sun began its descent. Glancing at her phone on her charging dock, she saw it was nearly five. Pushing the sheets aside, she strode through the bedroom toward the spacious bathroom. Moira turned on the shower before pulling off her bra and panties. She sighed as the hot water cascaded over her, waking her up the rest of the way.

Reaching for her favorite body wash, her mind thought back to the handsome man she had spotted at the restaurant bar earlier that afternoon. Moving the washcloth over her body, she couldn't stop the delicious and heated images that flickered through her imagination. From what she had seen, he looked to be strong and tall. A whimper escaped her when the soft soap lathered cloth danced over her nipples. God, she needed to be laid. Shaking her head to clear her lustful thoughts, she quickly finished her shower.

Grabbing one of the fluffy towels, she deftly wrapped her hair up turban style before reaching for the other towel to dry off. Once dried, she draped the towel over the rack and walked nude back into the bedroom. Roxi had told her to have fun while on St. Lucia and that was exactly what Moira planned to do.

Finding the dress, she had bought specifically for this trip, she carried it from the closet and lay it at the foot of the bed.

***

Moira slipped from the Uber at the curb of the restaurant. The place wasn't fully packed yet, but she would wager in an hour and half it would be. She moved to get in line and that's when she saw him. The man from earlier, standing right in front of her. He was currently dressed in tight jeans that hugged his ass deliciously. His shirt was green right now and he wasn't wearing his ball cap. Moira licked her lips as she drank him in, hoping he would turn around. As if fate heard her wish, the man turned. His hazel green eyes met and locked on with hers. Then he smiled.

"Hi there," he said.

"Hi." Moira grinned, feeling herself fight back a shiver at the sound of his voice.

"You American?"

"Aye, born and raised in D.C. You?"

"Was born in Charlotte, but currently live in New York. Oh, where the hell are my manners. I'm Cord. Cord O'Brien." Cord replied extending his hand.

"Moira Donovan." Moira said, placing her hand in his.

Cord frowned a second, "Donovan? Wait a sec, you're not Moira Donovan the author, are you?"

Moira giggled, "I am."

"I'll be damned. What a small world. So, you here alone or..." Cord let the question hang.

"I'm alone. My parents and brother bought this vacation for me as a treat for finishing my latest book. Well, the rough draft anyway." Moira stated. *'Why the bloody hell did I tell him that?'*

"I'm here alone too. My brother and partner insisted I take a vacation while one of our bars is being renovated. Since I haven't been on vacation in forever, I figured why not." Cord said with a shrug. "Would you care to join me?"

Moira was a bit floored. She didn't know this man, yet she really wanted to keep talking to him. Not to mention he had her feeling rather warm now. Nibbling her bottom lip, she thought it over.

***

Cord

Cord stood there with bated breath as Moira mulled over her answer. He hoped to God she would say yes. When he had seen her behind him, he just had to talk to her. She was even prettier up close. That gorgeous red hair was pulled up in a high ponytail. She was dressed in a curve hugging dress of kelly green that hooked around her neck, leaving her shoulders bare. The dress stopped about mid-thigh. She wore no makeup, and simple silver hoops at her ears. Then there were her eyes. They were the most amazing shade of blue he had ever seen.

"Well, what do you say? Join me for dinner then maybe dancing at this place I know." He asked again.

"Aye, alright Cord. I'll join you." She answered.

'Christ that accent of hers.' Cord groaned silently, as he offered her his arm.

She giggled a little before slipping her arm through his. The sound shot straight to his crotch. How the hell did this woman he didn't know affect him like this? Before he could think of anything to say, they were being led inside and to a table for two on the veranda. Being the gentleman, his mom had raised him to be, he held out her chair for her and helping her sit, before taking his seat across from her.

"It's refreshing to see that chivalry isn't completely dead." She teased.

"My mom raised me and my brother right." He replied proudly.

They were silent for a few moments as they looked over their menus. Their waiter appeared and both placed their drink and food orders. Once alone again, it was Moira that spoke up, "So, how did you end up from North Carolina to New York?"

"It's called college." Cord chuckled. "I went to Columbia and fell in love with the city."

"I can see that. I've been to New York a few times and I enjoy it. I went to NYU myself."

Their conversation paused when the waiter returned with their drinks. As she sipped her beer, Cord watched the low lighting filter over her features. Her face seemed to light up when she spoke. He wanted to learn more about this enigmatic woman across from him. "Your accent, I'm trying to place it."

"Irish. My parents were born and raised in Belfast, Northern Ireland. They came to America during all that mess with the UFV and the Provisional IRA. My Da is a Garda...I mean a cop for DC Metro and my mum is a nurse at George Washington University hospital. Me brother Sean, he's a Marine. He got out after serving eight years. He and his wife, Laura and their two kids live in Norfolk, Virginia." Moira explained.

In turn, Cord talked about his family. He explained how he and his brother came to be business partners. She laughed when he told her about him and Collen growing up in North Carolina. She got a soft look in her eyes when he talked about his parents and how even after all this time they acted like newlyweds. When their food arrived, their conversation continued. Cord couldn't remember the last time, if ever, he had enjoyed a woman's company like this.

CHAPTER THREE

Moira sighed as she and Cord slipped into the chairs at their table. After an entertaining and delicious dinner, Cord had brought her to the club they currently sat at. It was crowded but not overbearing. She looked over at Cord and smiled brightly. For the last three hours he had intrigued her more and more. Of course, two beers at the restaurant and two more here didn't hurt. He was smart, funny, and hot as hell. A girl couldn't ask for a better companion for the night.

"You're a pretty good dancer." He said, before lifting his beer to his lips.

"You're not so bad yourself Cord." She winked, taking a sip of her own beer.

Cord reached over and took her hand, sending shivers shooting through Moira, making her gasp slightly. Her blue eyes locked with his. She could tell he felt the same electricity that she was feeling. His lips curled in a smile as his thumb began rubbing lazy patterns across the back of her hand. Moira let out a shuddered breath, then licked her lips. What was this man doing to her? She opened her mouth to speak, but no words formed. With that hot smile still on his face, Cord pulled her back to her feet and led her to the dance floor as a sultry song began playing. When he pulled her flush against him, she bit back a whimper. The hard planes of his body pressed against her, lighting her Irish blood on fire. As he led them in their sultry dance, her mind went into overdrive.

She could almost picture how they would look together. Him strong and large over her, her body under him, writhing for his touch. Would he be a good lover? Her eyes meeting his again, answered her internal question. Oh yeah, he would be an exceptional lover. Cord pulled her tighter against him and she felt him. Hard and throbbing against her. She felt her panties grow wet at the contact. He leaned down and nuzzled her neck. This time Moira couldn't stop the moan that escaped her.

"You smell delicious Moira."

"Cord."

He lay a soft kiss against the pulse of her neck and she felt her knees start to buckle. His strong arms bore her weight and kept her upright and pressed against him. Moira lifted her head and had all of three seconds to register what he had planned before his lips took hers. His kiss was enthralling. Overwhelming her senses. Slowly her arms came up and around him, her fingers sinking into his hair as she kissed him back, adding her own heat to the mix. She felt him growl into the kiss when she rolled her hips into him, feeling him more against her.

She had never been this way before; let alone with a man she had only met three hours ago. Yet the way he held her and kissed left her wanting more.

***

Cord

Cord was on fire as he continued kissing Moira. From the moment he saw her that afternoon she had called to him. Like a Siren of myth. Now that she was in his arms he just wanted more.

He pulled away from her lips allowing them both to gasp in air. The song had changed but he kept them moving to their own song. Lust was a living breathing thing between them. Clawing viciously under his skin. He wanted this woman.

"If I'm being too forward say so, but fuck Moira, I want you." Cord hissed in her ear.

"Aye Cord, I want you too." Moira moaned back, her body undulating against his.

"As much as I want to take you to my place right now, I'm not sure we should. Hell, we barely know each other." He sighed.

He saw the lustful look in her eyes as she nodded, "You're right. Though I'm sure we both wouldn't regret it if we did."

Cord chuckled, "I wouldn't." He gently pulled away from her arms and led them from the floor. He saw her confused look as he led them toward the door. "Tell you what, I'll give you my number. And say tomorrow evening, you call me, and we'll make plans."

"Plans?" Moira questioned, tilting her head as she pulled out her phone.

"Yes plans. While I want to take you to my bed immediately, I'm not one of those men who has a string of one-night stands."

"Ah, now I understand. Alright, I'll give you my number but only if you give me yours."

Smiling, Cord nodded and handed her his phone. There in the glow of the streetlights they exchanged numbers. After she handed his phone back, he hailed her a taxi.

"Moira, text me when you get back to your condo. I had fun tonight." Cord said, opening the door.

"As did I. Thank you for an amazing first night." Moira beamed before kissing him softly.

Once she was in the taxi he waved as the car pulled away. Cord let out a long breath and turned to hail his own taxi. Fifteen minutes later, he was just walking into his condo when his phone dinged.

Made it back safe and sound.

Good. You can never be too careful these days.

Aye, true enough. Well, good night Cord. I'll text you tomorrow and we can make plans.

Good night Moira. I look forward to seeing you again.

Cord plugged his phone in and stepped out onto his deck. He breathed in the night air and let his thoughts wander. Who would have thought when he agreed to this vacation that he would meet an Irish siren?

***

Moira

Moira awoke to island birds and a gentle breeze blowing through her condo. As she stretched, the events of the previous night came drifting back. She felt herself smiling as she remembered Cord. Their conversations over dinner and how it felt when he held her and kissed her.

'Bloody hell, he was a woman's walking wet dream.' She thought slipping from the king-sized bed.

Grabbing the light robe from the foot of the bed, she practically floated out the French doors in the bedroom onto the deck. The morning was beautiful. The soothing sounds of the ocean washing ashore mixed with the birds was something she had only written about. Twenty minutes later, armed with coffee and her laptop, Moira sank into one of the comfy deck chairs. The events of last night and waking up to a magical island morning, she was feeling inspired. She opened her laptop and loaded up her writing program and within minutes she was typing away.

For over two hours she sat on the deck writing away. She paused as her phone dinged. Glancing over, she couldn't help the smile she felt expanding over her face. Sitting the laptop aside, she picked up her phone. It was Cord.

Morning. I know we said we'd text later, but I had to at least tell you good morning.

Good morning Cord. Hope you slept well. I know I did.

I'm glad to hear that. So, what are you doing right now Moira?

Moira giggled. She reached for her coffee and saw it was empty. With cup and phone in hand, she rose from the chair and walked back into the condo. As she waited for the coffee to reheat, she replied to Cord. *At the moment, I'm getting a coffee refill. I woke up and felt inspired. The last two hours I've been on my deck writing.*

Inspired huh? What inspired that gorgeous mind of yours?

A few things I think of like the ocean air, the island beauty...

And?

Moira nibbled her lip as she poured the coffee. Should she tell him that he was probably the biggest inspiration? Not just in her writing that morning, but the previous night he had taken center stage in a very erotic dream scape. Armed with a full cup of coffee she returned to the deck and sat down again. Debating a few more moments, she decided to just go for it and tell him. What the hell right?

You.

***

Cord

Cord sat on his own deck reading Moira's answer. He knew he had to be grinning like a fool but so what. An internationally best-selling author just said he was her inspiration. What red blooded man wouldn't be flattered. Taking a sip of his own coffee, he started typing.

So, I'm your inspiration huh? I think I like that.

:) What can I say, after last night I had plenty of...inspiration to choose from.

Cord couldn't stand it, he had to hear her voice. She answered after the first ring, "What exactly did you have to choose from Moira?

"Hmm, now why should I tell you Mr. O'Brien?"

"You know you want to tell me as bad as I want to hear you tell me." He chuckled.

Moira giggled and lord, the sound shot right to his dick. *"I suppose I could tell ya' a little. Last night I dreamed about you. That you continued what you started at the club on the dance floor."*

"Believe me baby, I wanted to. I dreamed about that last night too. Imagining what it would feel like, us being together." Cord replied, his voice deepening.

"Mm, I think I like that you dreamed of me too." Moira sighed.

"Damn woman, I want to see you. Right now."

"I'll text you my address."

Before Cord could say another word, she dropped the call. He stared at his phone in shock but then her text came through. He wasted no time. He stood from his deck chair and walked inside. Placing his coffee mug on the table, Cord picked up his wallet and condo keys and was out the door. He saw that her condo was only two lots over from his. If that wasn't fate, then he had no idea what was. In under ten minutes he stood on her stoop and knocked. Moira answered a few moments later.

When she opened the door, Cord just stood there drinking her in. That amazing red hair was twisted up and held in place by one of those clip thingies that women liked. She was wearing a strapless sun dress that clung to her beautiful curves and flowed down her body to stop at her ankles. It looked to be soft and a blue that matched her eyes. God this woman was beautiful. Smiling, she moved aside in silent invitation. He accepted and walked inside.

Moira closed the door and Cord made his move. He gave her only a moment to gasp before he hauled her up into his arms and kissed her.

Moira moaned as her arms and legs wrapped around his shoulders and waist. Taking two steps forward, Cord pinned her against the front door. She moaned into the kiss and deepened it. Cord groaned as he felt her body moving against his. Somehow, he pulled his lips from hers and started a slow path of kisses down the column of her neck. His tongue tracing lazy patterns against her skin, making her shiver.

"God, Cord..."

"You taste just as delicious as you did last night Moira."

"You too."

With painful restraint, Cord slowly began to lower Moira back to her feet. Sliding her body against his on the way down, leaving her with no doubt that he damned well wanted her. First and foremost, however, he was raised to be a gentleman. Taking a woman, one he barely knew, against the front door of her beach condo was not gentlemanly. Once Moria was back on her feet, he took both her hands in his and kissed the backs.

"I want you Moira, trust me, but...hell my mom raised me to respect women. And screwing your brains out against your front door wouldn't qualify." He explained.

***

Moira

Moira could not help but smile. "It's nice to know men like you still exist. Well, what do you say, we have some coffee, head out to the deck and talk some more?"

"Sounds like a plan." Cord nodded.

Moira decided she liked him holding her hand, so when he released them, she reached out and took one of his, and led him through the condo toward the kitchen. They fixed their coffee and walked toward the deck, Moira making sure to keep his hand in hers. He had such strong hands. They were the hands of a man who understood the meaning of work and not some pansy paper pusher.

"Okay, there's something I want to know." Moira began

"Okay." Cord nodded for her to continue.

"Last night when we met, you asked if I was the author. How in the bloody hell did you know I was an author?"

Cord laughed. "You can blame my mom for that. She has every book you've written. I've read your suspense series but haven't read any of the others yet."

Moira leaned back in her chair a little, "Well, that's a bit surprising. I only say that because you're not my target reading audience."

"I figured that much." He chuckled. "You told me you were writing this morning, what were you writing if you don't mind me asking."

"Oh no, I donna mind. I was continuing another romantic suspense project. I'm not sure when I will want to release it, but it's something I've been working on between my last release and the book I sent to my editor right before I came here."

Just like that, Moira found herself telling Cord a bit about her current project. As she talked, she was internally shocked at how easy it was to talk to him about her writing. Outside of her publishing house and her mom, she tended to find it difficult to talk about her writing process. Yet with Cord, the words just flowed, and he seemed to be genuinely interested in what she did. After she finished, he went on to talk about his seven bars and the work he and his brother Collen did. She listened as he explained how Collen handled the behind the scenes business while Cord was the front man for all seven bars.

"That's fascinating. And what kind of bars are they? I mean what is your typical clientele?" she inquired.

"We don't have a specific clientele in mind. All seven of O'Brien's Tap has a little something for everyone. Our most popular one is the one in Manhattan. It's also our biggest location. We have tourists, politicians, socialites, and celebrities. I spend maybe about half my time there." He explained.

"Is it your favorite location?"

"No, my favorite is the bar in the Bronx. I don't know why, but I love going to that one. Maybe because it's more down to earth. The people who frequent that one is about ninety percent locals."

Moira glanced over at her phone, "Wow, it's already lunch time."

"No wonder I'm suddenly famished. What do you say we go out to get some food then maybe do a little sight-seeing?" Cord suggested.

"You're on, but lunch is my treat today and I won't take no for an answer Mr. O'Brien." Moira challenged.

"Far be it from me to argue with a fiery red-head." He teased.

"Oh boyo, you have no idea how fiery I can be." She winked.

CHAPTER FOUR

Cord

Cord held Moira's hand as they walked among the other tourists and locals. He had to admit, he thoroughly enjoyed the feel of her hand in his. *'Oh, who the hell am I kidding, everything about this woman entices me.'*

Cord bit back a groan as he watched her bend over a table in the marketplace to examine something. When they left her condo, she was still wearing that body clinging sun dress and as she bent over, it clung even tighter to her ass. He moved so that he now stood directly behind her. Unable to stop himself, Cord pressed into her. He felt Moira stiffen for a moment but when her head turned and she saw it was him, her body relaxed. Moira cast him a mischievous smile as she slowly righted herself. Cord hissed as her body pressed against him as she leaned against his chest.

"Christ woman..."

Moira giggled turning to face him, "I told you boyo, you have no idea how fiery I can be."

Lifting onto her tiptoes, she pressed her lips to his. Her tongue gliding against his lips and just as quick as the kiss started, she ended it. With a wink and another giggle, Moira slipped from his arms and moved on to the next stand. Cord had to take a few calming breaths before he rejoined her side. While his body was semi under control, his mind was not. Thoughts and images of what he wanted to do to this woman bombarded him.

For nearly an hour they walked amongst the different shops and stands. When they left her condo, they had grabbed lunch at the place he had seen her at for the first time. Now as the sun began its transition into evening, Cord had brought Moira to a secluded stretch of beach near his condo. He spotted an area enclosed on three sides by a grouping of palm trees and sat on the soft sand, tugging Moira down so she now sat across his lap.

"Mm, you are so beautiful." Cord whispered, brushing her hair from her shoulder before kissing it.

"Such a charmer." Moira sighed, tilting her head slightly.

***

Moira

Feeling Cord's arms around her, his lips gently teasing her skin was driving Moira crazy. Last night had been interesting, but today was on a different level. During their excursion through the village, Cord couldn't seem to keep his hands from touching her in some way. Not that she was complaining. She liked it. A lot, and by the saints, she was really loving what he was doing to her now.

"You seem to enjoy touching me."

"I can't seem to resist you."

Moira sighed as his hand moved from her waist and cup one of her breasts. She felt her nipple pucker and her breast swell, as if trying to accommodate his hand. "I...I like you touching me."

"Good."

Moira moaned when his lips slanted across hers in a heated, commanding kiss. His hand began to knead her breast making her whimper and her back bow. His other hand moved from the small of her back to glide over her hip. She felt the skirt of her dress easing up her legs. When Cord's hand moved to cup her, she cried out, bucking into him. She was spiraling and she loved it and wanted more.

"Cord...what are you...doing?" she panted, her eyes meeting his.

"Touching you Moira." He breathed, pressing the heel of his hand against her clit. "Yes baby, enjoy it."

Moira couldn't find the words. Her eyes remained glued to his. Those green hazel eyes hypnotizing her. Her hips rocking against his hand, her hands gripping the front of his shirt as her legs opened wider. "I've never done something like this..."

"What do you mean?" he questioned, keeping his movements slow.

"Being...teased by a virtual stranger..." she paused on a moan and swallowed hard. "Wanting you to...not stop."

Moira nearly screamed in delight as she felt him ease her panties to the side and slip a finger deep inside her.

***

Cord

"Fuck me Moira...you're so wet." Cord growled into her ear, pumping his finger in and out of her. When she began riding his hand, his finger started moving faster. "That's it, Moira. Ride my hand. Let go for me."

He watched her as she didn't hesitate and bucked faster. Her hands were fisting his shirt, her blue eyes wide and trained on his face as he watched her. She looked beautiful in this moment. A flush staining her neck and cheeks, the soft mewling and whimpers that escaped her had him rock hard. Fuck he wanted to just lay her back in the sand and bury his cock deep inside her. But no, not yet. Soon though.

"You're close Moira. Let go for me."

"Cord!"

The second she started to scream his name in her release, his mouth moved and covered hers swallowing the sound. His finger pounding deep as she rode out her release. As her body began to relax, his movements slowed as well. She moaned, almost in protest, when his finger slid from her body. Moira's eyes opened; the blue orbs glazed over. With her watching he lifted his finger to his lips and sucked. Moira licked her lips as she watched him. Cord moaned at her taste and couldn't wait to taste her for himself.

"Yum. You taste delicious Moira."

"Christ, I donna think I've ever felt so turned on."

"Glad to know I do that for you." He winked, making her giggle. "I better get you back to your place."

***

Moira

Moira sat on her deck watching the moon rise over the ocean. Her laptop open to her latest project. After Cord walked her back to her condo, he kissed her softly and headed back to his place. She had immediately jumped in the shower and let the steam wash over her trembling body. After her shower, she slipped on a pair of comfy cotton pants and a tank top then pulled out one of the many delivery menus that were on the counter of the kitchen. She ordered her dinner and now, two hours later sat with a glass of wine writing.

She had texted Cord and let him know that once again he had been her inspiration for her current writing streak. He had seemed to like that and told her he was looking forward to more inspirational encounters. Moira sighed dreamily as she recalled the feel of his hands on her body. How she had reacted to him today and the previous night. Had any man ever made her feel this way? Her ex Phillip certainly hadn't.

Picking up her wine glass she took a sip of the sweet wine. After placing the glass back on the table, she went back to finishing the scene. She had every intention of sending it to Cord once she was done. Once the scene was finished, she copied it and emailed it to herself before using her phone to send it on to Cord.

Thought you might enjoy a peek at what you inspired today. :)

***

Cord

Cord sat at the bar of a cantina when Moira's text came through. He had invited her out again tonight, but she declined saying she was a bit tired from their day out. He understood and said for her to text him the next day. Lifting his beer, he opened her text. As he read the scene, he was both awed at the talent she possessed and the reaction her word had on him. It was quite a heady feeling knowing he was the inspiration for the words he now read. Finishing reading, he immediately texted her.

Wow, that was amazing. Would I be too forward in saying it made me hard knowing I inspired this?

I would be disappointed if you weren't Cord. ;)

Cord chuckled; *you are an incredibly talented writer. Can't wait to read the whole story you're working on. Especially if this scene is in it.*

You just might receive an advanced copy?

I hope I do. My mom would be jealous. :)

Cord finished his meal, paid his bill, and rose to leave. He moved outside and started making his way back to his condo. The night air was fragrant with a mix of sea air and florals. It was cool compared to the balmy heat of the day, the sky was clear, and a full moon and millions of stars illuminated the sky. When he reached his condo, he moved around the back and glanced over toward Moira's. He spotted her sitting on her deck. The light from inside her backdrop, casting a faint halo around her silhouette and the light from her screen lighting her face.

I hope you had fun today Moira. He texted, walking back to the front door.

I had an amazing time today. I look forward to seeing you tomorrow. I have a list from my friend Roxi of things and places I have to go see and do while I'm here. Lol.

Then tomorrow we'll get started on that list. Good night and I'll see you tomorrow.

Good night Cord and I look forward to tomorrow as well.

Cord laughed heading for the bedroom. He needed a cold shower, or he would never fall asleep. The scene she sent him was her recreation of what had happened that afternoon on the beach. He sighed remembering how wet she had got for him. How her body moved against him, the way her eyes spoke volumes of how good she had been feeling in that moment. The cold water sluiced over him but did nothing to lessen his raging erection. Growling, Cord gripped himself and as his hand moved, his mind imagined it was Moira's hand. Or better yet, Moira's mouth.

As his hand moved faster against his skin, his imagination ran rampant. Imagining him burying himself hard and deep inside Moira. In moments he came, hoarsely calling out Moira's name. Fuck he had it bad for this woman and hoped soon they both would feel that completion of being together. Trembling slightly from both the coolness of the water and the intensity of his orgasm, he soaped up and rinsed off. He exited the shower, dried off and threw on a pair of boxers. Now feeling exhausted, he climbed into bed and with his last conscious thoughts of the woman a few doors down, he fell into a lust filled slumber.

***

Moira

Moira stood nervously, "Um, are you sure this is safe?"

Cord grinned and tightened the straps around her waist, "I promise you Moira, this is perfectly safe. I've done this lots of times."

Moira took a calming breath and nodded. When Roxi had given her the list and Moira saw zip-lining, she had some trepidation about it. Yet, this morning when she told Cord about it, his face had lit up like a schoolboy on Christmas morning. She decided to "bite the bullet" as they say and go for it. Now she stood on a wooden platform, wearing a contraption around her waist and upper thighs that was supposed to keep her from plummeting a few hundred feet to the ground.

Beside her, Cord stood similarly rigged up but unlike her, he looked excited and ready to go. He turned to look at her and as if sensing her nerves, he took her hand in his and lifted it to kiss the back of it. This offered her some strength and as one, they moved to the edge of the platform. Moira paid close attention to the instructions the operator was giving. How to sit, how to push off and more importantly, how to stop. The last thing she wanted while on vacation was to break her bloody neck on some stupid zip-line.

"You ready Moira?"

"I...as ready as I'll ever be."

"Trust me, the hardest part is stepping off. I'm right here with you. We'll do it together. One. Two. Three!"

On three, she and Cord pushed off the platform. The moment she was in the air, all fear vanished from her and was replaced with exhilaration. She heard herself whooping in thrill as she and Cord sped along the line toward the ground. When they came to a stop, she turned laughing at Cord. His hair was windswept and his eyes bright with the excitement she too felt. She impulsively took his hands and pulled him toward her before kissing him.

"Can we go again?"

"Anything you want baby." Cord grinned.

***

Cord

Cord sat across from Moira at the table of the restaurant they were dining at. It had been on Roxi's list. After their thrilling zip-lining adventure, he had taken her to lunch at his condo. He remembered her look of surprise when he offered to cook. He told her his mom had made sure both he and Collen could not only cook but sew and a few other things that had once been classified as "women's work".

"Okay, so you can cross zip-lining off the list, as well as Martha's Tables." He said.

"Aye. And after dinner you said we were going to The Cane Bar correct?" She questioned.

"That's right." He nodded. "How's your food?"

"It's delicious. I swear in only the four days I've been here I feel like I've gained twenty pounds."

Cord threw his head back and laughed, causing her to laugh along with him. Cord found himself looking for ways to make her smile or laugh. Whether it was tickling her, he found that one out by accident on their second day together, showing her something new and exciting, complimenting her or just holding her hand. While he enjoyed those things, it appeared that Moira enjoyed it just as much. That made him want to do it even more.

"Hope you have your dancing shoes on. I plan on holding you on the dance floor tonight."

"Oh, I have me bróga damhsa on."

"Huh?" he asked.

Moira giggled, "Bróga damhsa is dancing shoes in Irish. My parents made sure me, and Sean knew how to speak Irish just as fluently as we do English. Da says we should be proud of our heritage. We are American aye, but we're Irish too."

"I hope you'll share more of that Irish with me." Cord smiled, lifting her hand to his lips.

"Hmm, if you're a good boy I might." Moira grinned, before lifting her glass to her lips.

"Well, let's go dancing." Cord stated.

After dropping some money on the table to cover their meal and tip, he took her hand and steered her outside. He quickly hailed a taxi and in moments they were off toward the club. When he had picked her up and caught that first glance of her outfit for the evening, he wanted to just say screw it and take her to his bed instead. Moira was wearing a black and green corset top that plumped up those mouth-watering breasts of hers. The corset stopped about an inch above her bellybutton. She also had on tight low-rise jeans, which hugged her hips and ass in the most sinful and delicious way. The look was topped off with black heeled boots. How in the hell was he supposed to keep from fucking her blind after tonight, he had no idea?

CHAPTER FIVE

Moira

Moira moved against Cord as they danced. No matter what song played, he was the perfect lead. The second she stepped into his arms her body seemed to instinctively follow. In that moment, a slow romantic ballad filled the bar. Sighing, she rested her head against him.

"You having fun?"

"Oh aye. Since meeting you I've had more fun than I have in a long time."

She felt his finger under her chin, lifting it. In the low light she saw a gleam in his eyes that heated her. When his lips came down on hers, she pressed tighter against him.

Damn his body felt good against her. She knew if she told Roxi about this her best friend would be shocked. After the mess with Phillip, Moira had become more than a little standoffish when it came to dating. For Christ's sake she hadn't had sex in nearly a year, come to think of it.

Yet with Cord O'Brien her heart, mind and body seemed to agree it was time to throw caution to the four winds and just have a little fun for once.

"I think I'd let you kiss me all night." She breathed.

"I'd love to." He grinned.

***

Cord

He walked them back to their table and ordered them another round. "So, what's on the agenda for tomorrow?"

"I honestly don't know. I'll look over the list when I get back and let you know tomorrow."

"Fair enough," he nodded. He cleared his throat before speaking again. "Moira, I want you to know that this...you and me I mean, well... I've never been like this with other women. It's a first for me."

"'Tis the same for me. For nearly a year I've not done much in the lines of dating. Partly because the last year has been busy on the writing front. I had six author events, three releases and two book tours."

"And the other reason?"

"The other...well, that's a bit complicated. Let's just say I went through a bad breakup."

Cord took her hand and squeezed it gently. He wouldn't push even though he really wanted to know what happened. He hoped her ex hadn't been one of those asshats that liked to beat up on women. Men like that deserved to be dragged through the streets and shot as far as he was concerned. Moira Donovan was the type of woman that deserved to be kept and loved. Emotionally and physically.

"I see. Well, since we're both here for three weeks, what do you say we just enjoy our time and see what happens?" He proposed.

"I say, you're on Mr. O'Brien." She answered brightly. "You can start by dancing with me some more."

"It will never be said that I don't aim to please." Cord smiled.

***

Moira

Moira laughed as Cord broke the surface sputtering. "How do you like it?"

"I at least gave you warning." Cord countered, wiping the water from his face.

"Like bloody hell you did." She laughed, splashing water at him.

That morning she had awakened to a text from Cord asking her to go swimming with him after breakfast. She agreed. She had fallen in love with the ocean when she was about seven and her parents had taken her and Sean on vacation to Myrtle Beach, South Carolina.

"You're a sneaky one."

"I have an older brother and I'm Irish. Of course, I'm sneaky."

Moira let out a squeal just as Cord grabbed her and wrapped her in arms. "I can be sneaky too Moira."

"Thanks for the warning." She giggled.

The giggle faded into a moan when he kissed her. She hadn't been lying the night before when she said he could kiss her all day. As he continued his assault on her mouth, she vaguely registered being lifted into arms and him walking toward the shore.

When he eased her down against one of the towels they had brought, she sighed. His body rested partially over her, so he wasn't crushing her. It felt both comforting and sizzling.

"Have I told you how fucking sexy you look in that bikini?" Cord asked, his voice deepening.

"No, but I'm glad you like it." Moira answered, her fingers slipping through his wet hair.

Cord kissed her once more before lying beside her, pulling her to him so she was nestled against him. "What's on your agenda for today?"

"Well, I was thinking of actually spending the day writing. I've been on such a roll with the latest project, I want to strike while the iron is hot." She replied, hearing sadness in her voice.

***

Cord

Cord moved onto his side, shifting Moira onto her back once more. "You sound sad about that."

"Well, I donna want you to think I donna want to spend time with you..." she began, but a finger to her lips stopped whatever she had been about to say.

"Baby, you don't have to explain anything to me. Nor do you have to worry about hurting my feelings. Writing is your livelihood and I'm not going to stand in your way."

She lifted a hand to caress his cheek. "You're too good to be true Cord O'Brien."

"I could say the same about you Moira Donovan." He replied, turning his head to kiss her palm. "What do you say I take you back to your place. Then, if you want, we can meet for dinner. I could even cook for you again if you'd like."

"That sounds wonderful. Should I go to your place or mine?"

Cord thought for a moment. "I'll come to you. Any requests or you want me to just surprise you?"

"Surprise me." Moira beamed.

After escorting Moira back to her condo, Cord returned to his own to grab a shower. He then decided to grab a little nap before he did some shopping for dinner.

***

Cord

Cord awoke from his refreshing nap and began thinking about what he could make Moira. Since they weren't in the states, his mom's famous chicken fried steak was out. Well, he would just go into the village and see what jumped out at him.

With his mind made up, and a plan, Cord left his condo. The marketplace was bustling. All around him was a cacophony of not just noises but delicious smells. Moving through the various stalls he eyed the produce and such. Sadly, nothing seemed to be jumping to mind.

"You seem confused."

Cord turned to find an older woman standing next to him. "Actually I am. See, I met this amazing woman four days ago and well, I really like her. I offered to cook dinner at her condo and I'm drawing a blank."

The woman chuckled, "I see. Are you a decent cook?"

"I'm no Wolfgang Puck, but I know my way around a kitchen." Cord grinned.

"Follow me. I have a recipe at home I think will be perfect."

"Thank you." Cord breathed in relief. "I'm Cord O'Brien."

"Amelia Ledoux." Amelia smiles accepting his offered hand.

***

Moira

Moira sighed as she saved her work. Today had been productive with her story and with any luck, it would be finished soon. As she rose to stretch, heavenly smells wafted from her kitchen. Her stomach growled in anticipation. Gathering up her laptop, she carried it into the bedroom.

"Buíochas le Dia that smells good." Moira all but moaned as she walked into the kitchen.

"I'm guessing that's more of your Irish?" Cord grinned, stirring something on the stove.

"It means 'oh my god.' What are you making exactly?"

"I was at the market-place, completely at a loss as what to make you. This older woman, I'm guessing she's someone's grandma, took pity on me. She took me to her house, wrote down a recipe and sent me on my way." Cord explained.

Sitting on one of the bar stools, Moira cupped her chin, "Another woman you say. Should I be jealous?"

Cord laughed, "No baby. Her name is Amelia Ledoux and she has to be in her mid-sixties."

"Well, if whatever she told you to cook tastes half as good as it smells, I want to meet her and say thank you." Moira replied.

"I agree." Cord nodded, turning off the burner.

As Cord began putting the meal in the serving dishes, Moira started setting the table. She also pulled out the bottle of wine Cord brought to go with dinner. Moira studied him as he began serving up their food. Making sure her plate was fixed before his own. She found it refreshing. Today, too many men have forgotten what it means to be a gentleman. Although, given the way Cord kissed her these last few days, Moira had a feeling that in bed he wouldn't be the gentleman.

"This looks really delicious Cord."

"I think I followed Amelia's recipe correctly. Well, let's dig in."

Moira lifted the first bite and the moment the food touched her tongue, a moan escaped her. The burst of flavor was out of this world. The meat was super tender and flavorful. The multiple layers of seasonings and spices worked in harmony with one another. When her eyes reopened, they met Cord's and she smiled.

"Okay, tomorrow you and I are tracking Amelia down and thanking her for this recipe."

"Oh yeah." Cord nodded.

"What is this called again?" Moira questioned.

"Amelia told me that the locals call it pepper pot. She said this was her grandmother's variation of it." Cord explained.

Moira lifted another bit to her lips, once again moaning her satisfaction. "I am so going to have to copy it before I head home. My mum and da would love this. So, would me brother Sean and his wife Laura."

Cord reached into his pocket and pulled out a folded piece of paper and handed it to her, "Amelia wrote out a copy for you. She said she hasn't met anyone, local or otherwise that hasn't enjoyed this dish."

Moira took the recipe and smiled at him. "Yes, we are thanking Amelia tomorrow."

After dinner, Moira and Cord cleaned up, grabbed the bottle of wine and were now currently sitting on her deck. She was curled into his side, her head resting against his shoulder and one of his strong arms draped comfortingly around her. The last lights of the sun fading into the deep blue and violet hues of the encroaching nights. Watching the stars come out to twinkle and sparkle and the moon beginning its ascension was peaceful.

"I think this island is probably the second most beautiful place I've ever visited." She sighed.

"What's the first?" he asked, laying a soft kiss against her forehead.

"Ireland. When my grandparents died, we all went back to Belfast. Sean was about eight I think, and I had just turned four. I'll admit I donna remember much, but I remember how green it was in the church yard. I plan to someday soon travel Ireland and see all its beauty for myself." She answered.

"I've been to Ireland before. A year after we opened our first bar, two of my bartenders were invited to the Jameson Bartenders Gathering. I was able to go along with them. Dublin was a busy yet beautiful city."

"I've only seen pictures of Dublin. My Da says his nephew is living there now. Maybe if I ever get over there, I'll look him up."

Feeling Cord holding her to him, his fingers lazily grazing her upper arm was so soothing. It had been a long time since a man had made her feel this relaxed. She leaned forward and placed her empty wine glass on the table. She watched as Cord tossed back the last of his wine and put his glass beside hers. He shifted his hold and moved her, so she sat across his lap. She smiled softly, moving her arms around his neck, teasing the fringes of his hair with her fingers.

"You look happy right now."

"I am Cord. You've made me happy." She whispered before leaning in and kissing him. "Not just today, but since that first night we met."

Cord pressed his lips to hers again, cupping her face in his hands. "You've made me happy too Moira. I've never met a woman who's had me as fascinated as you. I don't know who to thank for our paths crossing."

"The Catholic girl in me says, thank God, but the Irish in me says maybe the fae folk have a hand in this too."

"The fae folk?"

"Aye. Tuatha Dé Danann. They are creatures of Irish mythology. Ethereal beings of an advanced race that lived eons ago in and around Ireland. It's said they sometimes intervene with us wee mortals to their amusement or sometimes they see something that mortals don't."

"I don't much give a damn who is responsible, but I thank them all the same."

"As do I Cord. As do I."

CHAPTER SIX

Moira

Moira's eyes opened and a moment of confusion hit her. She was in her condo, but she was laying on someone's chest. Taking a breath, the masculine smell she smelt brought the previous night's events back to her. After dinner she and Cord had sat on her deck for hours just talking, kissing, and enjoying each other's company. At about one in the morning they came inside and the last thing she remembered was curling against him on the couch.

"Morning babe,"

Moira giggled, tilting her head up to find Cord's green hazel eyes studying her. "Morning yourself."

"How did you sleep?"

"I slept wonderfully. What about you? I wasn't too heavy, was I?"

"You too heavy? That's funny. I liked sleeping with you in my arms."

Moira nibbled her bottom lip a little, "I know I'm not super skinny..."

Cord stopped her by hauling her up and over him. Moira gasped, her legs widening as she now straddled him. "Moira, I know you are not trying to say that you're fat."

"Well, not fat, but I have some curves..."

"And I love your curves."

To prove his point, Cord ran his hands up her legs, along the curves of her hips to come to a stop at her waist. Moira shivered under his touch. "I like your touch."

"Good. Now, mind explaining what bullshit you were about to say about you being too curvy?"

She sighed. Should she tell him? Oh, what the hell, why not. "I mentioned before about a bad breakup. His name was Phillip. The first year, things were fine but somewhere around year two..."

"It started to go to hell?" he asked.

"In a big way aye." She nodded. "Suddenly, things that he never seemed to have issues with became a big thing. He's a political journalist and I went with him to several political events. About six months before we broke up, I accompanied him to a congressional dinner. I was coming back from the bathroom and I overheard him talking to one of the congressmen. Phillip said that I was a bit curvier than he would like to be showing off, but what could he do."

***

Cord

Cord was floored at what Moira had just told him. "He actually said that about you?"

She nodded, sadness and pain reflecting in her eyes. "Aye and the congressman actually laughed and told Phillip that he understood seeing as his own wife was in the same boat."

He sat up and wrapped his arms around her. To Cord, Moira was the most beautiful woman he had ever met. She was built the way he believed a woman should be built. Her hour-glass figure drove him crazy and haunted his dreams with imaginings of what she would feel like naked and bare beneath him. When he pulled back a little, he placed a finger under her chin, lifting it so their eyes were level.

"Moira, your ex is a dumb-ass. You are perfect just the way you are, curves and all. All I can say is that his loss is my gain." Cord stated.

Before she could speak, his head lowered and captured her lips with his. His hold around her tightened, pouring every ounce of his want and need for her into the kiss. In seconds, Moira was moving against him. With her straddling him, their bodies were intimately touching, and he felt his cock swelling as her hips rocked, pressing herself against him. His fingers tightened against her hips while growling.

"Fuck Moira. You're driving me crazy."

"Good, now you know how I feel every time you kiss me."

*****

Moira

Moira didn't give Cord a chance to speak. Her mouth took this time. She was the one doing the taking and controlling of the kiss. Before now, Cord had been in the driver's seat and damnit, she wanted to drive. Her hands pushed against his chest, and she followed him as he lay back against the sofa. His hands slid from their position at her hips upward along her spine, sending electric shocks through her. Those strong fingers of his tangled in her hair and tightened. This only served to make her wilder and she began grinding against him, both panting harder.

"Cord...I..."

"I know Moira. Let go for me. I want it."

She let go and cried his name, her eyes never leaving his. She wanted him to see what he did to her and she wanted to see his lust in his eyes. She wasn't disappointed. Those gorgeous multi-colored eyes of his burned with need. Need for her. Shivering in the aftermath of her climax, she lowered against him. Under her cheek, she felt his heart hammering like hers was. Between her legs she felt him throbbing. She had her release, but poor Cord hadn't. Well, Moira would just have to fix that. Lifting her head to gaze at him, Moira slowly started shifting down his body. It took him a few moments for his mind to register what it was she was intending to do.

"Moira, what are you doing?"

"I think you know boyo."

"Oh my god..."

*****

Cord

Cord was on cloud nine. He had a beautiful woman on his arm, it was another beautiful day in paradise and said beautiful woman had given him the hottest blow job he'd had in…well forever if he were honest. He had been surprised when she had moved down his body and, in a fluid, motion opened his jeans, pulled him out and went to town on him. Of course, it hadn't taken him long to come and she surprised him further by swallowing him all.

"You alright over there?" Moira teased, a knowing smile.

"It's your fault my mind keeps replaying this morning." Cord shot back.

"That means I did my job." Moira winked.

"Cheeky wench." Cord grumbled, then started laughing.

He and Moira were walking through the Union Nature Center. Around them flowers bloomed as they moved down the hiking trail. With each passing day he spent with this woman, he wanted to know more and more about her. He wanted to know more about her family, her passions, and any other scrap she'd throw his way. Yes, he had learned a lot about her, but he was thirsting for more. He wondered if she felt the same about him.

About an hour later, he and Moira were back in the village looking for somewhere to eat lunch. Cord turned and spotted Amelia. He practically drug Moira over to the older woman. "Hello Amelia."

Amelia looked up and smiled, "Well hello there."

"Moira, this is Amelia Ledoux. She's the one who gave me that recipe." Cord introduced.

"It's nice to meet you. I told Cord that we had to find you and say thank you." Moira smiled, offering Amelia her hand.

"I take it you enjoyed the stew." Amelia chuckled, shaking Moira's hand.

"Aye, it was delicious. I can't wait to try it when I get back home for my parents. We meet every Sunday for dinner. I know my Da will love it." Moira nodded.

"What have you two been up to today?" Amelia questioned.

"We just got back from seeing the nature center. Now, we're trying to decide where to have lunch." Cord answered.

"Why don't you two come home with me and I'll fix you up something." Amelia suggested.

"Oh Amelia, we don't want to impose…" Moira began.

"It's no imposition dear. I insist." Amelia argued.

Just like that, Amelia led Cord and Moira away from the market toward her house. Cord hadn't had the chance to really pay attention to the house the day before, but he did now. Amelia's house was charming. It was an older style island bungalow. Open, airy, and well maintained. Amelia told Cord and Moira to have a seat at the breakfast nook in the kitchen as she set about preparing lunch.

"Now Moira, tell me a bit about yourself." Amelia said.

"I'm an author. I write romance and romantic suspense."

Amelia paused and studied Moira a bit more closely, "Wait, you're Moira Donovan. Now I recognize you. I own several of your books. You are an exceptionally talented writer."

Cord found it sweet when he saw Moira blush slightly at the older woman's praise. It appeared that Moira wasn't used to being recognized by her readers unless perhaps she was at some author event. This endeared her even more to him. Despite her success as a writer, she wasn't jaded by it. As Moira and Amelia got to know each other, he just sat there beside Moira taking in the scene before him.

***

Moira

Moria felt blissfully exhausted as she exited her shower. After spending the day with Cord visiting the nature center and then lunch with Amelia, Cord had dropped her off at her condo and then headed to his own. She never would have imagined when she took this trip that she would meet someone like Cord, let alone the feelings that were beginning to develop for the bar owner. He checked off all her boxes in what she wanted in a man. He was smart, successful, caring, handsome, and unselfish.

She slipped on her cotton pajamas and headed for the kitchen for a glass of wine. After Cord dropped her off, she ordered take-out and did a bit more writing as she ate. Now, with a glass of wine she walked out onto the deck to enjoy the evening. In the far distance she saw flashes of light, indicating a storm rolling in. Her thoughts were interrupted by her phone. Glancing at the id, she saw it was her mom. Smiling, she answered.

"Hello mom."

"Hello M'inion. How are you enjoying St. Lucia?"

"Oh Ma, I'm so glad you, Da, Sean and Laura picked this place. It's so beautiful and magical at the same time. The flowers here are amazing and then there's the food. Speaking of food, I got a recipe from a local woman I'm going to cook for you and Da. It was delicious and I know you two will love it."

Maureen laughed, *"I'm glad you're enjoying yourself. I know you took your laptop, have you done any writing?"*

"Aye, I've been working on that project I told you about a few months ago. This place has been such an inspiration." Moira answered.

She opened her mouth but paused. She had almost told her mom about meeting Cord, but something inside her told her not to. It wasn't like Moira to keep secrets from her mom, but for some reason she couldn't quite bring herself to speak about Cord. She listened as her mother talked about what was going on back in DC, fighting the gnawing guilt that was trying to creep in. No, she would tell her mom about Cord, but not now. Maybe when she got home, she would.

"Have you and Da made anymore plans regarding your retirement?" Moira asked, changing the subject.

"No, not really. Your Da and I still have a few more weeks before we have to submit anything final. I promise you darlin', once we decide we will tell ya' and Seany." Maureen laughed.

Moira and Maureen chatted for a few more minutes before Maureen said good night and hung up. Moira sat there sipping her wine thinking over her decision to not mention Cord O'Brien. Was she afraid her mother wouldn't approve? No, it couldn't be that. Her parents had always supported her choices, and this would be no different. The best Moira could figure, it was that more along the lines of fear of self-sabotage. Almost as if she spoke of the amazing time, she was having being with Cord would ruin it somehow.

When she heard the first rumblings of thunder, she decided it was better to head in. She picked up her phone and wineglass and walked inside. Not ten minutes after returning inside and closing the windows, the first drops of rain started. Standing at the deck doors, she watched the storm roll in. Since she was a child, Moira had loved watching storms. There was something magical about the lightning, thunder and rain swirling together. The anger, the violence and yes, the beauty of it was a perfect symphony. When the storm was done raging, the world always seemed cleaner and fresher somehow. Turning from the doors, Moira moved to the couch and picked up the book she had brought to read and was soon lost in the book as the storm raged outside.

CHAPTER SEVEN

Cord

Cord stood outside the shop where he and Moira had agreed to meet the night before. For the last week now, he and Moira had spent every day together. Either he went to her condo or she went to his for breakfast and coffee. After that, they would walk through the village just taking in the sites. A few days ago, Moira had told him about the list that her friend Roxi had given her of things to do and see on the island. So far, they had checked off six things from the list. They were planning on hiking through Pigeon National Park and exploring Fort Rodney.

Moira had told him she loved hiking. During college, she and Roxi had gone hiking whenever they had the chance. Cord had responded telling her that his family loved being outdoors. Hiking, camping, fishing, whatever they found time to do. He was looking forward to the hike. He had arranged for a picnic lunch to be delivered to the fort and it would be waiting for them after the hike. Today would be their third hike on the island.

"Cord."

He looked up to see Moira walking toward him. "Hey. How are you this morning?"

Moira leaned up and kissed his cheek, "I'm good. I canna wait to see this trail. Roxi says it's beautiful. I've seen the pictures she took the last time she was here and they're breathtaking."

Cord smiled and draped his arm around her shoulders, resting it on her day hike pack. As he led her toward the bus waiting to take other tourists to the trail head, he told her what he remembered of the trail. He loved how her face illuminated as she absorbed the information. They filed onto the bus and within minutes were on their way. The whole ride, he held her hand and she didn't seem to be in any hurry for him to let go either. This pleased him more than he cared to explore at the moment.

"Um, Cord?"

"Yeah?"

Moira fidgeted a little next to him as the bus rumbled along, "Well, I'm just curious but, have you told your family? About meeting me and all?"

Cord shifted so he could face her better, "No. Why, have you told yours?"

"No, I haven't. I guess...bloody hell." She sighed, "Cord, so far this last week has been amazing. I suppose I don't want the bubble to burst."

"I know what you mean there. Moira, I've had so much fun with you and I'm looking to have more fun," he smiled, leaning in for a sizzling kiss. The kiss was short but still hot. He pulled away and smiled at the hazy look in her blue eyes. "For now, whatever this is between us it's no one's business but yours and mine. Okay?"

"Aye. Only ours." Moira nodded slowly, smiling lazily.

***

Cord led Moira through the lush island forest. About two hundred yards behind them a large group of tourists were following their guide. This wasn't Cord's first rodeo, so he told Moira they didn't need a guide. She smiled and followed his lead. "Want to see something fascinating?"

"Aye." She grinned.

"Come on, you'll love this."

Taking her hand, Cord gently pulled her toward their right into the forest. A few moments later as they stepped into a clearing beside him, he heard Moira gasp at what lay before them. Half buried under the vegetation of the forest were several stone ruins. Cord watched as Moira stepped away from him to get closer and examine them. The pure wonder on her beautiful face was a joy to see and he knew he was right to show her this.

"Oh Cord. This is incredible."

"There are ruins like this scattered along this trail and a few others on the island. Some are from the days when there was an active fort here and others are believed to be from the first islanders that inhabited the island before Europeans came here."

"There is so much history here on this tiny island." She smiled, pulling her camera from her pack.

"Yeah there is. Kind of like Ireland." He replied.

She threw a smile over her shoulder at him before turning back to take pictures. Cord studied her as she walked among the ruins, snapping pictures left and right. Rays of sunlight piercing the canopy above them seemed to envelope her, glittering off her red hair, making it illuminate like fire. He couldn't wait to see first-hand what all that glorious red looked like spread against his pillow.

***

Moira

Moira was amazed at the beauty that she saw around her. She and Cord were now at the peak of the mountain where Fort Rodney rest. Off in the distance she could make out the island of Martinique. Below along the cliffs, the ocean washed and crashed along the shore and rocks. When they reached the end of the hike, Cord had surprised her again with a waiting picnic lunch. As she ate one of the sandwiches, she studied the man beside her.

Not only was he handsome, wealthy, and smart, he was also one of the sweetest men she had met in an exceedingly long time. He seemed almost too good to be true. He was the complete opposite of her ex, Phillip. Phillip had been consumed with work and making a name for himself as a political journalist. At the beginning, things had been nice. He had seemed interested in what she did but that hadn't lasted long. By their second year together, he was only interested in what he wanted to do and his career. By year three, Moira had had enough and left him.

"Hey, you okay?" Cord asked, breaking through her thoughts.

"Huh?" Moira questioned.

"Where were you babe, you looked a million miles away."

"Sorry, was just woolgathering, as my Da would say. I'm still trying to take all this in."

Cord pulled her to him and situated her in his lap, his strong arms cocooning her. "You're beautiful. All of this is just window dressing."

Before she could say anything, his lips descended on hers. Jesus, Mary and Joseph the man could kiss. Moira pushed all thoughts of Phillip and the past away and surrendered to this man who held her so securely. She shifted so her arms could wrap around him as she returned Cord's kiss. God above she wanted this man. Wanted to feel him drive her crazy. She whimpered at the feel of one of his hands tease the side of her breast. Her nipples puckering in confines of her bra.

"Cord…"

"Moira, you feel so good in my arms."

"I like being in your arms."

"Good."

With one more heated kiss, Cord released her. She let out a sad sigh, but knew with them being in public like this, they really couldn't do more than kiss. She slid from his lap and watched as he went to work packing up the remains of their picnic. Ten minutes later, they were making their way back down the trail to catch the bus back into town. Moira was so lost in her lustful thoughts; she didn't notice right away that Cord had taken them off the main trail and into the forest.

"Um, Cord? We're not on the path anymore." She pointed out.

"I know." He grinned wickedly.

Moira barely had time to gasp before Cord was kissing her again. This time, the kiss was pure lust. She moaned feeling her panties growing wet. His tongue slipped between her lips and began thrusting in and out. Her body trembled in need and her knees threatened to give out. Cord began walking them and Moira found herself braced between the hard planes of his body and a tree. Moira whimpered as she felt one of his hands slide between them to cup her through her khaki shorts and now soaked panties.

"God above."

"Shh. We're not that far from the trail Moira."

Her hips began bucking as his hand started sliding back and forth, causing delicious friction. "Yes Cord."

"I want to feel you baby." Cord hissed in her ear before nipping it.

She was lost.

***

Cord

Cord stood there watching Moira buck against his hand. He needed to feel her. Now. Deftly, his hand undid the button of her shorts, then pulled down the zipper. His hand slipped inside her shorts and he palmed her. Christ she was hot, and her panties were wet. Kissing her again, he managed to move the cloth to the side and slipped a finger inside her. She cried into his kiss as he growled. She was soaked and tight.

'Fuck me. She's going to feel so good around my cock.' He thought hazily adding a second finger. "That's it Moira. Ride my fingers."

"Cord...yes..." Moira gasped, clinging tightly to him.

Cord's eyes stayed glued to her face. Watching those lustful emotions play out for him. Her eyes were closed, her head tilted back against the tree. Her back bowing as her hips undulated a little faster and harder. Grinning, he began pumping his fingers faster and deeper. Her mouth opened to form a perfect 'O'. She was close and he wanted her to reach her climax. He leaned down and started kissing and lapping at her neck, urging her to come.

"Cord...I'm going..."

"Yes Moira. Come for me. Now."

Cord's lips captured the scream that erupted from her as she exploded in his arms. Her petite body trembling against his as her climax surged through her. Her juices coating his fingers and most of his hand. His cock throbbed painfully in his jeans, wanting release of its own. Soon, soon he would find release. As Moira calmed, his kiss slowed, and he finally pulled his lips from hers. Those blue eyes of her fluttered open and locked on his.

"My god, that was amazing."

"And that's only the beginning."

"Your condo or mine?" Moira asked, before nipping his bottom lip.

"Who fucking cares as long as there's a bed." Cord moaned.

"Then let's go." Moira giggled.

"Yes ma'am." Cord grinned.

***

Cord

Cord somehow managed to get them through the door of the bedroom. It was a bit difficult with Moira in his arms wrapped around him like a damned boa constrictor. The moment they got off the bus, he hailed a taxi and they were on the way to his condo. They walked inside and the moment Moira dropped her pack, Cord had her up in his arms kissing her for everything he was worth. Moira had responded and was moving her body against his. Now in the bedroom, he lay her on his bed and untangled himself from her arms and legs.

"I want you naked Moira."

"Aye, but only if you join me."

Moira sat up and whipped off the t-shirt she had worn. He licked his lips seeing her full breasts in a silver bra. Reaching for the hem of his own shirt, he yanked it up and off and without taking his eyes off her, went to work on his jeans. Moira smiled seductively as she kicked off her shoes and pulled off her shorts. Cord hissed when his jeans and boxers brushed against his erection. The Irish beauty before him was in only her silver bra and matching panties.

As he fumbled with kicking off his shoes, he kept his eyes locked on the red-haired siren laying on his bed. He growled when she smiled and cupped her breasts. When he rose back to his full height to shove down his jeans and boxers, Moira licked her lips while pulling down the cups of her bra.

"Christ woman you're driving me insane."

"I like that I drive you crazy."

***

Moira

Moira felt like her heart was about to burst from her chest when she saw Cord naked for the first time. He was an Adonis in the flesh. Hard, lean and muscles in all the right places. Her eyes roamed him from head to toe then back again. When he gripped his erection, she moaned and tugged at her nipples.

"You look so fucking amazing Moira." He hissed.

"Cord, I want you. Please." She breathed.

Cord didn't make her wait any longer. He was on the bed and kneeling between her legs in seconds. Moira barely managed his name before he yanked her panties off, and his mouth was on her.

Moira's eyes rolled up into the back of her head and her back bowed off the bed. The feel of his mouth on her and his tongue deep inside her was bliss.

"Cord...oh my god yes."

All she heard from him was a hum of satisfaction. Glancing down her body she found him watching her. Her hips bucked, grinding her clit against his mouth. With a moan she somehow managed to unhook and toss away her bra. Cupping her breasts, a little rougher, she kept watching Cord go down on her.

"Bloody hell!"

Her orgasm hit her hard and fast. Her body seized as she exploded for him. His mouth and tongue however refused to relent. She could barely breath as he pushed her toward release again. Moira screamed in rapture when he added two fingers along with his tongue.

"Damn baby, I could eat you all night." Cord smiled, moving up her body.

"I... donna...think I could survive it." Moira panted.

"Let's see if you'll survive me inside you then."

***

Cord

He was halfway over her when reality pushed through his lust. Hauling himself off the bed, he rushed to the bathroom. Digging in his toiletry bag, he pulled out a strip of condoms. He tore one off and turned back for the bed.

Moira's gaze was confused and changed to recognition when she saw him rolling the rubber on. He rejoined her on the bed, his body looming over hers.

"Now, where were we?" He asked.

"I believe you were about to test my survival skills." She teased.

Cord chuckled then kissed her. He took hold of her hips, elevated them, and began easing inside her. He knew how tight she was, and he wasn't exactly little. Both groaned as the first inch slipped into her.

"Moira...you're so damned tight."

"More Cord. I want more."

How the hell was he supposed to say no to that? Lifting her up so her ass now rested on his thighs, Cord pushed forward more.

Her muscles clenched around him, forcing him to hold back the need to just drive himself home. While she was tight, her two orgasms eased his way and in moments he was balls deep.

"Fuck." He gasped.

"Don't stop now." She pleaded, her legs wrapping around his waist.

That was all it took. Cord fused their lips together as he started to move. As much as he wanted to make love to her, he knew they were both too far gone for that. Feeling her nails drag along his back and her body moving in tandem with his thrusts spurred him on.

"Fuck me Cord. Now."

"I'm not going to last. Moira, I want you...with me."

"I'm there. Now Cord."

Hearing the lilt in her voice deepen was the last push he needed. Gripping her hips, he thrust harder. Once. Twice. On the third he roared her name as he came, Moira's cry mingling with his as she joined him in orgasmic overdrive.

Cord slowly sank atop of her as the aftershocks rolled through him. Softly kissing the column of her neck, he could feel her pulse racing and her body trembling beneath him. Not wanting to crush her, he rolled so they were on their sides.

"Wow." He panted.

"I don't think I survived." She sighed, brushing her hair from her face.

Cord chuckled. He began to ease from her, causing them both to moan. On jelly legs, Cord rose from the bed and disposed of the condom then returned to Moira.

"Stay with me." He said

"Aye." She smiled.

He pulled the sheets back and they slipped under them. Moira curled into his arms with a contented sigh. Cord tucked her head against his shoulder and held her close. He wasn't finished with her. Not by a long shot.

CHAPTER EIGHT

Moira

Sunlight filtered into the bedroom as Moira slowly awakened. She stretched, feeling wonderfully sore. She reached over to Cord's side of the bed and found she was alone in the bed. Sitting up, she looked over and found a note on his pillow. She picked it up and smiled.

Moira,

Went for a run, be back soon. Oh, by the way...don't get out of bed and don't get dressed.

She had to laugh at his instructions. Was he nuts? She had no intention of getting out of bed. Laying back down against the pillow, she reflected on the events of last night. After their first and entirely too fast round one, Cord had taken her again after a short nap. The second round was just as hot but much more leisurely. She didn't think there was a single part of her body that Cord hadn't touched, kissed, licked, or tasted.

The third time had been all for Moira. She had flipped the tables and it was her turn to have her way with Cord. She had taken her time in touching, tasting, and teasing him just as he had her. It had made her so hot when she would feel him shiver and moan her name when she touched or licked a particular area. Cord had nearly come unglued when Moira had finally taken him in her mouth. Even now as she remembered it, Moira's body heated up. Closing her eyes, one of her hands eased down between her legs.

"Mmm, Cord."

Moira was soon lost in the memories of the previous night and she never heard the door of the condo open and close. She slid two fingers inside, her legs widening under the sheets. She was quickly getting wetter and while her fingers felt good, they were a poor substitute for Cord. Her haze was disturbed when the bedroom door moved, and her eyes opened to find Cord standing there wearing a hot as hell smirk watching her. His skin glistened in a sheen of sweat from his run.

"Starting without me?"

"Sorry, not sorry."

"Well, in that case don't let me stop you. You keep up your work and I'll be right back after I rinse off."

Moira nodded and watched him enter the bathroom. When she had seen him at the door with him watching, it felt so naughty and made her excited. The same way she had felt when he had fingered her on the trail yesterday and on the beach a few days before that. Not knowing if they were absolutely alone added a touch of excitement and naughtiness. Her hips started moving slowly in tune with her fingers. Each slid inside as she reached a little deeper. Not knowing what Cord had planned, she wanted to make sure she was more than ready for him.

"Fuck me you look amazing Moira." Cord stated, exiting the bathroom. She opened her eyes and just watched him walk toward her. "Seeing you fingering that sweet pussy, laying in me bed wanting me."

"I do want you Cord. Please." Moira sighed, never taking her eyes from him.

***

Cord

Cord was entranced with Moira. The thin sheet clinging to her naked form, the tops of her breasts barely covered and the hardened nipples poking through the sheet. He could see her legs open wide and her hand moving slowly between them. It was obvious that she was trying not to build her release up too fast. Those blue eyes he adored were watching him, pleading for him to touch her, kiss her, hell do something to her. Cord kneeled beside her on the bed.

"Are you wet my Irish rose?"

"Aye...aye I'm wet for ye."

He gave the sheet a tug, exposing her breasts to him. He had to taste her. His head lowered and he sucked one of the hardened peaks into his mouth, making Moira gasp his name. Cord shifted on the bed and slid one of his hands under the sheet and joined her hand between her legs. While she continued the slow thrusting of her fingers, he found her clit and started teasing it. Feeling it swelling under his finger.

"That's it, baby, rock your hips."

"Cord..."

"You're wet now. I can't wait to feel my cock deep inside you again."

Moira couldn't even form words and only groaned in agreement. When he started moving his thumb faster over her clit, her fingers started moving faster, matching his speed. Cord wanted her to come once before he took her again. Last night she had been a wild woman and he wanted her that way again. His head moved to the other breast and his free hand reached up to palm the breast he had just abandoned.

He felt his cock stiffen as Moira's moans and mewls grew louder. She was close he knew, and he wanted her to hit that peak. In moments, she cried his name as her body rocked with shivers. Cord felt her juices flowing from her and wanted to be inside her right fucking now. He reached for the nightstand and pulled out a condom packet. He quickly ripped the foil open and once he was covered, rose over Moira.

"I can't wait anymore baby. I need you." He hissed.

"I need you too Cord." She nodded.

Pressing his lips to hers, Cord eased himself into her wetness. Moira wrapped her arms and legs tightly around him as he sank into her. His growl deepened when he suddenly found himself on his back with Moira now rising over him. Her fingers lacing with his she began grinding slow and hard against him. Cord gasped, tossing his head back against the pillow, rolling his hips up to match the pace she was setting now.

"Fuck Moira, that's it. Ride me baby. Take me deep."

"Fuck me back Cord. Oh, I love you deep."

Cord lost himself in the woman above him. When she sped up, he matched her. As Moira came down, he thrust up hard, driving him deeper each time. Cord looked up watching Moira, as she slowly lost herself. That moment he felt his orgasm begin, he gripped her hips and flipped their positions again. Pinning her wrists above her head, Cord started pounding into her. She had a vice grip around him, and he couldn't get enough of her and wanted her to come once more. To come with him.

"Fuck me Cord. Don't stop." She begged, squeezing her legs around him taking him.

"Come again for me Moira. Come with me." He gritted, pistoning faster and harder. His climax hit him like a sledgehammer. His body locked up as he emptied into her. Beneath him, Moira's back bowed as she clenched around him, taking everything, he was giving her. She was a beautiful sight when she came for him. In the back of his mind he wondered what it would feel like without the thin layer of rubber between them. He suspected if it felt this good with the condom, without one would damn near kill him.

'But it would be a hell of a way to go.' Cord thought, as he eased down over her.

***

Moira

By midafternoon, Moira was back at her condo sitting on the sofa with her laptop. After the blissful night and morning with Cord, she was full of both inspiration and a little trepidation. As she typed away, her thoughts ran wild. What was happening between her and Cord? Was this just some hot, wild island fling? Was it more? Moira had never been one for casual sex, unlike Roxi and a few other friends who had no compunction with having one-night stands.

'What is this connection between us? Am I falling for him?' she wondered, finishing her paragraph. She saved her work and closed her laptop. Standing, she picked up her glass of tea and moved onto the deck. *'He's such an incredible guy. Smart, handsome, and a hell of a lover, but is that enough for a relationship?'*

Sighing, she stared out over the water. While they had more in common than just an animalistic need to jump each other's bones, there was the matter of geography. She lived in DC and he in New York. True there was only a distance of maybe three hours, but could they make it work? His job was in New York, his brother was there. He had told her that his parents still lived in North Carolina but visited often. She had had one long distance relationship before, and it hadn't ended well.

In high school, her then boyfriend had gone off to UCLA and she had gone to NYU. For a year they tried to make it work but it ultimately ended with him meeting a fellow biology major and ended things. She had later learned he had been seeing the other girl for nearly six weeks before he broke up with her over an e-mail of all things. After that, Moira swore she would not do a long-distance relationship again.

'But would it really be a long-distance? You could visit him, and he could visit you.' Her mind argued.

***

Cord

While Moira thought over where they stood, Cord himself was in the same boat over at his condo. Like Moira, he too hadn't had much luck with long distance relationship and was leery of trying again. Yet there was something about Moira Donovan that he couldn't just push out of his head. Or his heart. He was pretty damn sure that he was falling, if not already fallen for the Irish woman.

'Could we make it work somehow once we get back to the states? DC isn't that far from New York really.' He thought, lifting his coffee mug to his lips.

It had been years since he had been in a serious relationship. While he wasn't a man-whore, he wasn't a celibate monk either. He wouldn't call them one-night stands per se, but it wouldn't be far off. With Moira though, he wasn't just thinking about sex. Sure, they were hotter than hell together, he wanted more with her. He enjoyed just being with her. Talking, spending time with her. That was more of a connection than he had had with a woman in a long time.

'I think over the next week and a half she and I need to talk and see where we stand with each other. If I have even half a chance of building something, I want to explore it.' He decided.

When Moira had left his place, they made plans to meet up for dinner at around six. Tonight, at dinner, Cord would take the chance and put himself on the line with her. He just prayed to God that she was on the same page or at least willing to explore their options. Polishing off his coffee, he re-entered the condo and started preparing for tonight. He was walking over to her place, then they would walk into town and grab a bite.

***

Moira

For some reason, Moira felt nervous. She had taken her time in getting ready for dinner tonight. She washed and fixed her hair, was meticulous with her makeup and spent nearly two hours agonizing over what she was going to wear. Finally deciding on a halter style sapphire blue knee length dress, she and Roxi had bought for this trip. After her writing session that afternoon, she had made up her mind to talk to Cord at dinner to see where they stood with each other. If she was merely a vacation fling, she would accept that. Her mind was a bit divided, however her heart was sure that Cord felt the same things she was feeling for him. She had just finished slipping on her heeled sandals when the doorbell rang.

'The man is nothing if not punctual.' She grinned, grabbing her purse, and walking to the door.

She opened it to find Cord standing there, holding a bouquet of colorful flowers. He was dressed in a button-down short sleeve dress shirt of hunter green that went perfect with his eyes. Instead of the jeans or khaki shorts he typically had been wearing, he wore black slacks. His look was topped off with a pair of black, polished boots. Overall, the man was sex and sin on legs, and he was hers. For the moment at least.

"Wow, you look beautiful." Cord gaped, looking her over from head to toe. "I thought you might like these." He added, presenting her the flowers.

"They're beautiful Cord, thank you." She smiled, then inhaled the fragrant flowers, her eyes closing in enjoyment. "Come in while I find something to put these in."

She led Cord inside and walked toward the kitchen. She found a green ceramic vase hidden in one of the cabinets. Filling it with water, she placed the flowers in the vase and carefully arranged them a little before taking the vase over to the table and sitting it in the center. She turned and was immediately pulled into Cord's arms. Moira giggled. Cord smiled and leaned in to kiss her. Moira sighed. Unlike their previous kisses over the last week, this one just felt different. She couldn't put her finger on it, but everything in her being told her tonight was going to change things between them one way or another.

"That's a good start to the evening." She said, her voice sounding breathy to her.

"And the night is still young. So, you ready?" he replied, looping her arm with his.

"Aye, let's go." She nodded.

Arm-in-arm, Cord lead them from her condo. The night air was cool, clear, and filled with the fragrance of the different flowers that always seemed to fill the nights here. She would have to ask Amelia what they were and maybe see if she could get them to grow back home. That way, regardless of how things went with her and Cord, at the end of this trip, she would have the scents to remember their time together. Hopefully, if what her gut told her was right, tonight would mark a new start for her and Cord and not the end.

CHAPTER NINE

Cord

They were quickly seated at the restaurant. After making his decision to take her to dinner, Cord had quickly done a search and found the perfect place to bring her. He got lucky in getting a reservation and a semi-private table. The conversation he knew they would be having needed as much privacy as he could muster. When he saw where their table was, he was pleased. They would have the privacy they needed. Cord pulled out her chair and pushed it in for her before taking his seat across from her.

"What can I start you two off to drink?" the waiter asked.

"I think I'll start off with a peach tea please." Moira answered.

"I'll have the same." Cord nodded.

The waiter smiled and walked away. "This place is beautiful Cord. How did you manage to get reservations on short notice?"

"I got lucky." Cord winked. "I..." he paused a moment, regathered his thoughts and spoke again. "Moira, I feel you and I need to talk before things go any further between us. I felt a place like this would be perfect."

Across from him he watched Moira's face and saw the various emotions play over it. He saw nervousness, understanding, hope, and a hint of fear. The fear worried him. He never wanted to hurt her or have her fear him. He reached across the table and took hold of her hand. He wanted to erase that fear. He watched her lick her lips before she spoke.

"Aye, I agree Cord. We do need to talk. I won't deny a part of me is a bit scared, but I hope you and I are on the same page."

"Baby, from what I'm seeing on your face, I believe we are. Let's order first, then while we wait, we can talk. Okay?"

"Alright."

The waiter returned with their drinks about five minutes later and they quickly placed their orders. Cord could sense that, like him, Moira wanted to get this conversation done and over with. Once alone again, Cord took a deep breath and kicked things off. "Moira, I don't know about you but this last week or so has been beyond amazing. We've had fun and I don't know if you've felt it too, but I just feel like there's this deep bond between us. I've never felt anything like it with any woman."

"Yes, I have felt it too and like you, I've no' felt this with anyone. No' even with my ex, Phillip. I feel as if we can talk about anything and everything. You seem genuinely interested in what I do, and I find what you and yer brother do fascinating."

"I am interested in your writing. Hell, everything about you I find interesting. You're always on my mind. I find myself wanting to know what makes you smile, laugh, your fears, your dreams." Cord paused when the waiter brought their appetizer. He squeezed her hand and continued. "Moira, I'm ninety-nine-point nine percent sure that I'm falling for you. I know that's crazy seeing as how we've only known each other what...a week? Week and a half? But there you have it."

Cord studied Moira's face. He saw what looked like tears in the corner of her eyes and he hoped like hell they were happy tears.

"Oh Cord. I donna think I could've said it any better. I'm with you. We are on the same page. I know it's crazy seeing how we hardly know each other. Well, outside of the bedroom. I know I'm fallin' for you too and I want to explore whatever this is between us."

Cord lifted their joined hands to his lips and pressed soft kisses to her knuckles, "Baby, I'm glad we're seeing eye to eye here."

"Me too. I know we still have more to work out, but we still have another week or so before we head back to the states. That's plenty of time to figure out the rest. Right?"

"Very much right. Now that we have the heavy part finished and we know where we stand, let's start our appetizers and enjoy the evening." He smiled.

"Yes. Let's enjoy tonight." She nodded.

***

Moira

After dinner Moira and Cord left the restaurant and headed to a small club nearby. It was semi crowded but the patrons looked as if they were mainly locals. It was perfect. She watched as Cord walked back toward their table, carrying their drinks and her heart melted just a little more.

'He's the most amazing man I've ever met.' Moira thought, taking her drink from him.

"You looked like you were thinking hard there." Cord commented.

"More like admiring the view." she winked, before lifting her Mai Ti to her lips.

After Cord had admitted he was falling for her, he couldn't seem to keep his eyes or hands off her. Of course, you would never hear Moira Katherine Donovan complaining. Moira was in a similar boat not being able to keep herself from looking or touching him either.

Sipping her drink, she reached across the small table and took his hand in hers. Cord squeezed her hand as he sipped his beer. The low lighting of the club made his hazel eyes seem darker. The shadows playing around his face seemed to be doing wickedly delicious things to her.

"What are you thinking Moira?" He asked.

"I'm thinking how wicked you look in this lighting." She answered, her voice shaking.

She watched as Cord sat down his beer then took her glass and sat it down beside his bottle. Silently, he pulled her to her feet and led her onto the dance floor as a seductive samba began playing.

Moira felt her whole body heat up when Cord's arms enveloped her and pulled her flush against him. Feeling her body pressed up against his was something that just felt so natural to her. Almost as if instinctually, their bodies just knew one another. It was the same when he made love to her. He just seemed to anticipate her body's movements and reactions before he even touched her. For Moira it was the same with him. She seemed to know where he wanted her to touch him, kiss him, or just to tease him.

"What are you thinking?" he whispered in her ear, nipping at her lobe.

"Just how good it feels being in your arms." She sighed, shivering in delight.

"If I had my way you'd stay in my arms and in my bed." Cord stated, his eyes burning with his desire for her.

Moira moaned when he pulled her tighter to him and she felt him hard and throbbing against her stomach. Looking up, she licked her lips as she started rocking against him. When Cord growled low and deep, she felt herself get wet and knew if he were to slide his hand under her dress, he'd feel how wet her panties were. Feeling a little adventurous in the moment, Moira moved a hand between them. Keeping her eyes trained on his, she gripped his cock through his slacks and squeezed softly. They continued dancing as she stepped up her tease.

"Baby...what are you..." Cord panted.

"Just having a little fun." Moira winked.

***

Cord

Cord couldn't believe what was happening right now. Moira was in his arms and at the same time unbuttoning and unzipping his slacks. It took everything in him not to react when her small hand slipped into his pants and gripped his cock. He knew he was rock hard and judging from the look in those glowing blue eyes she liked that. He couldn't tell what was making him so hard. Was it having Moira in his arms? The fact that she was slowly jerking him on a crowded dance floor where anyone could see? A combination of both? Yeah, that was probably it, the adventurousness she was exhibiting in this moment.

He cast a quick glance around and quickly made a decision. Keeping in rhythm with not only the song playing, but also the rhythm of Moira's hand, he moved them into a secluded dark corner on the far edge of the dance floor. He spun them so Moira was now pressed between himself and the wall behind her.

Moira looked up at him. Cord could see the lust, excitement, nervousness, and love reflecting at him in her eyes.

"You're tempting fire Moira."

"And just what do you plan to do about it, boyo?"

His restraint snapped then and there. Her Irish lilt thickened, her breasts swelling under his gaze. Cord leaned down and captured her lips with his in a fierce kiss. Moira surrendered to him, her hand tightening and stroking him a little faster. Cord's hips rolled, matching her hand's speed. Cord had never done anything like this, and it exhilarated him. Moira moaned into their kiss, her back arching and her hand slowly slid from his pants.

"Cord...I...I..."

"You're hot and wet for me aren't you Moira? If I were to touch that sweet pussy of yours would I find it soaked for me?"

"Aye."

He wanted to see for himself. Pressing closer to her to better shield them for spectators, Cord moved one of his hands between them. Placing it on her thigh, he eased his hand up her thigh, sliding under the skirt of her dress as he did. Moira's eyes fluttered open and her breath hitched as she realized what he was doing. At the same time, she was doing nothing to stop him. In fact, her legs opened more giving him easier access. In seconds, Cord's hand was cupping her. He groaned feeling how wet she was.

"Christ woman, you're soaked."

"Aye, you look at me and I get wet."

"I want you Moira. Right now. Let's go."

"Please...I need..."

Cord studied her. Moira was trembling and her hips rocking, which caused her to press against his hand searching for friction. Hell, his pants were still open, and he was ready to go. Looking around he saw that they were well hidden by not only the corner but the low lights of the club. Cord held an internal debate for about thirty seconds before he decided. Gripping her wrists, he lifted them and pinned them above her head.

"Fuck it."

***

Moira

Moira had no chance to react before he was kissing her once more. With her hands pinned over her head, she was helpless, but she wasn't scared. Hell, she was turned on even more. With one hand pinning her wrists, Cord used his other arm to lift her off her feet and stepped into the v of her body. Moira immediately wrapped her legs around his waist. God, she wanted this man. Right then and there, to hell with the fact that they were in a public club. She was so wet and horny for Cord; she would let him fuck her in the middle of Times Square right now. Her lust fogged brain cleared for a second when she felt the head of his cock press against her.

"Moira?"

She knew what he was asking. She only had one answer for him, "Aye Cord. Please. Now."

With those words, she felt Cord thrust into her. Moira gasped as he filled her. His thrust was slow and steady, letting her feel every amazing inch of him as he filled her. She fought to stay still and quiet. Finally, he was balls deep inside her. After he thrust that last inch in, he groaned and buried his face into the crook of her shoulder, his grip on her wrists loosening enough for her to pull free and wrap her arms around his neck.

"Fuck me, Cord you're so deep." She panted into his ear.

"You're like a vice on my dick baby." He hissed, his hips starting to move.

Moira bit her lip to keep from screaming her pleasure. The feel of Cord thrusting in and out of her was the most amazing thing she had ever felt. This time however, it was different. There was a rawness to it. Cupping his face, Moira kissed him urgently. Trying to tell him what she wanted and needed. Luckily, Cord was so in tuned to her that he caught on. Holding her hips tightly, his thrusts became faster and harder. Moira wrapped her arms tightly around him and just held on as he pounded away. In less than ten minutes both Moira and Cord were hitting their peaks together. Moira couldn't remember ever coming so fast as she just had with Cord. In an instant though, the blissful moment was shattered. Cord's head snapped up, nearly clocking her in the process. When she looked at his face, she saw abject horror etched there.

"Cord, what's wrong? You look like you've seen a bloody banshee."

"Christ, I'm such an idiot."

"What are you talking about? You're no' making sense."

"Moira, I didn't use protection. "Cord blurted out. "God baby, I'm so sorry. I can't believe I didn't think…"

"Cord, stop." Moira stated. She softly cupped his face, "Cord, baby, it's alright. I'm on the pill. I haven't been with anyone in over a year. I had my yearly done a month before I came here. I'm clean and this is the first time I've never used protection."

Cord seemed to relax a little at her words, "I'm clean too and until just now I have never NOT used a condom. But I still should have thought of that and I should never have put you at risk."

"I understand how you feel, but I didna' give you much time to think straight." She giggled. "I will say though, now that I've felt you skin-to-skin, I don't think I'd want you any other way."

"You mean it? Because I'll tell you, you felt so good wrapped around me bare." Cord growled.

"Oh, I mean it. So, what do you say we get out of here and go back to my condo? This was fun, but I want more." Moira said, leaning in and nipping at his bottom lip.

"I say fuck yes." Cord groaned.

CHAPTER TEN

Cord

Cord slowly came awake as the morning sun poured into the bedroom. He turned his head and looked down smiling. Curled up against him, with her head over his heart, Moira lay there sleeping. Last night had been amazing. After their quickie in the dark corner of the club, they had come straight to Moira's condo and continued what was started. It had been nearly three in the morning when he and Moira had all but passed out.

He couldn't help himself, he reached out and softly brushed a long strand of her red hair from her face. After that first night they met, he had fantasized what it would feel like against his skin. Last night she had teased him mercilessly with her hair once she discovered he liked it. Cord slid his fingers into her hair as he leaned down and kissed her. He felt her shift in his arms and return his kiss. His body began reacting as she pressed into him, her arms sliding around him.

"Good morning baby," he whispered

"Good mornin' yourself," she smiled.

"How do you feel Moira? Was I too rough?"

Moira stroked his cheek, "Cord, last night was the most amazing night. You were phenomenal."

Cord felt himself relax. He had been quite unhinged last night. "I was a bit worried. I got a bit out of control that last time."

Moira surprised him and all but shoved him onto his back before straddling him. "Aye, you were." She leaned down and nipped his lower lip causing him to growl, "But I liked you out of control. You had your fun, now I'm going to have mine."

He quirked a brow but soon found out what she meant. He gasped when she gripped his erection and guided him inside her. She was wet and ready for him. Bracing her hands on his chest, Moira started moving over him. Cord moaned her name as he tossed his head against his pillow, taking hold of her hips. He kept his eyes locked on her. Moira smiled seductively as she took what she wanted. Him.

"Cord, you feel so good."

"I love being inside you Moira. I love everything about you."

"I love you too."

Cord met her halfway when she leaned in for a kiss. As their kiss heated up, Moira's movements became faster. Cord wrapped his arms around her and flipped their positions. Pinning her wrists over her head, he took control and drove deep. Moira's legs locked around him as she gave in to him. Cord wanted to feel her release first and thrust harder and faster. In seconds, she screamed his name as she tightened around him. He erupted then, groaning her name as he emptied into her.

"Bloody hell, that's a good way to start the day." She sighed as the tremors faded from them.

"I'll say it was." Cord agreed, rolling onto his back, pulling her into him.

"So, what are our plans for the day?" she asked.

"I'd love to spend the whole day right here, in the bed, naked and screwing like rabbits." He answered.

"I think I could do that. Think you can keep up?" she teased.

"You bet that Irish ass I can."

***

Moira

Moira stiffly slipped from the bed and moved toward the bathroom. Turning on the shower, she reflected on the day before. True to his word, Cord had kept her in bed naked all day yesterday. Before Cord, all day sex-a-thons were something she had only read and wrote about. Cord had not just fucked her, but also made love to her. She had many fans ask what the difference was. Moira had always answered the difference was the feelings involved. She now knew that it was more than that. When Cord genuinely made love, it was so different than when they just screwed.

When she stepped under the hot spray, she moaned as the water massaged away the stiffness. Hell, she could still smell Cord's scent clinging to her. She remembered how after her and Phillip would have sex, she would almost immediately grab a shower. But with Cord she liked his smell on her skin. Everything about the man appealed to her. Smiling, she shampooed and conditioned her hair before washing her body.

Twenty minutes later, wrapped in only a towel, she exited the bathroom and walked to the closet where she had hung up some of her clothes. Today, she and Cord had agreed to meet up for dinner. When he left earlier that morning, he told her to relax and have a day to herself. Moira selected an ankle length sun dress and a pair of flip flops. Twisting her hair up and clipping it into place, she glanced at the bedside alarm clock and saw it was nearly lunch time. Deciding to eat out, Moira grabbed her purse and keys and headed into town for a quick bite. Thirty minutes later she was seated in the very restaurant where she had first seen Cord sitting at the bar. She had just placed her order when her phone rang.

"Hello?"

"Hey girl. So, I see you're still alive." Roxi joked.

"Aye, alive and kicking."

"How are you enjoying St. Lucia? I told you you'd love it."

"I'm enjoying meself so much Roxi. It's amazing here."

"And the eye candy?"

Moira paused. Should she tell Roxi about Cord?

"Moira? Hey, you still there?"

"I met someone Roxi." Moira blurted out.

"WHAT? Okay. You've got to spill. Now."

And so, Moira did. She told her best friend about spotting Cord at the bar that first day and how the next evening they had dinner together. For once, Roxi remained completely silent as Moira told her everything that had happened and how much she was enjoying being with Cord. How they went sight-seeing together, dinners, dancing, and just hanging out. "I swear Roxi, I've never felt anything like this. Nor have I met someone who just wants to hang out like Cord does."

"Wow. He sounds like a helluva guy. You said he owns a couple of bars in New York?"

"Yes, O'Brien's Tap."

"Wait one damn minute. Are you talking about Cord O'Brien?"

"How do you know..."

"Hello! Moira, Cord O'Brien is one of Manhattan's most eligible bachelors. He and his brother Collen. Oh my god, my best friend is shacking up with..."

"Roxi, you can't say anything. You must promise me. Hell, I haven't even told my parents and I don't think he's said anything to his family either."

"Moira, I promise I won't tell a soul." Roxi paused, *"So, what are you feeling for him?"*

"He told me he was falling in love with me. I said the same. Christ Roxi, I love him."

"I'm happy for you. Lord knows you deserve someone after the shit that Phillip put you through. I don't want to put a damper on this but, he lives..."

"In New York and I'm in DC. Aye, we've brought that up and this is both of our last week. But New York isn't far. I could go visit him and he visit me, or even meet somewhere in the middle." Moira pointed out.

"That's true. Well, I'm sure you two will figure it out. When are you going to tell your parents?"

"I was thinking maybe today." Moira replied.

***

Cord

Cord put his plate in the sink just as his phone rang. "Hello?"

"Hey big brother. How's paradise?"

"It's amazing Collen. How are things at the bars?"

"Everything is going just fine. We're ahead on the renovations and the place will be ready to open back up Friday night. I figured you'd want to be here, so I pushed it back till Wednesday."

"No, go ahead and open on Friday." Cord said.

Collen was silent for several moments, *"Um, okay, who are you and what have you done with my brother?"*

Cord couldn't help but laugh, "Collen, I'm fine. Look, if I tell you something, can you keep it under your hat. At least till I get back?"

"You want me to keep something from mom and dad?"

"Just for a short time. I'm going to tell them but...damnit I must tell someone or I'm going to bust.

"Fine, I'll keep it quiet. It's not bad is it?"

"No, nothing bad. Collie, I met someone. No, not just someone, I'm in love." Cord rushed out.

Cord quickly and excitedly told his brother and best friend all about meeting Moira and all the things they'd been doing. He told Collen how everything about her just intrigued him more and more. How he couldn't wait to talk to her as soon as he woke up and that she was the last person he spoke to before falling asleep. "God Collen, I've never felt so connected to someone the way I feel connected to Moira. It's like, kinda like you and me but different at the same time."

"Moira?"

"Yeah, her name is Moira Donovan..."

"Wait one damned minute. You aren't talking about the internationally bestselling author Moira Donovan, are you? The one mom is nuts over?"

Cord chuckled, "The very same."

"I'll be damned. When mom finds out she's going to flip." Collen laughed. *"Does Moira know that you're a multi-millionaire and one of the most eligible bachelors in New York?"*

"I don't think so. Look, she and I still have some logistics to work out. I live in Manhattan and she lives in DC. All I do know Collen, is that I love her, and she loves me. The rest is details we'll figure out." Cord sighed.

"I hope it works out for you brother. Alright, I'll keep this quiet. When were you planning on telling mom and dad?" Collen asked.

"I don't know. I need to talk to Moira. Until today I haven't said a word to anyone. I don't know if she has yet or not." Cord answered.

***

Moira

Moira climbed out of the Uber and spotted Cord walking toward her with a bright smile. She felt herself smile as she moved toward him. When she met him, he pulled her into his arms and kissed her softly. Moira melted against him and wound her arms around him. Slowly Cord released her. He tucked her into his side and steered them toward the restaurant he had picked. Moira lay her head against his shoulder. Suddenly, a feeling of guilt settled on her. She drew a breath and started talking.

"Um, Cord, earlier today I...you see Roxi called and I kind of, well, I told her about you."

Cord stopped and turned so he was facing her. "You did huh? Well, I should confess and let you know I told Collen. He promised to keep it to himself for now. Will Roxi do the same?"

"Aye, she'll keep quiet. She also seemed to know a few things about you that I didn't." Moira replied.

"Oh? Like what?" Cord questioned, shifting a little from foot to foot.

"That you're an eligible bachelor and a multi-millionaire." Moira grinned, poking him in his chest. "You seem embarrassed boyo."

"Look, the money and notoriety are a huge pain for me, but it's helped my business, so I take it with a grain of salt. As for the money, I don't flash it around. I have the same truck I had back in college. The only splurge I've ever had was buying my brownstone. After I made my first million, I bought my home lock stock and barrel. After that I've kept my money in the bank. Made a few investments sure, but overall, I'm not some big spender, jetting off to casinos and stuff." He explained.

She reached up and cupped his face, "Cord, I didna need a breakdown of your portfolio. I got the feeling when we first met that you were very down to earth and over these last weeks you have shown me that. Like you I have money, course you knew that. I'm not a millionaire yet, but I'm well off. Money is not everything and I like that you are just you."

"Right back at you baby." Cord said.

"Now, let's eat." She smiled.

Moira and Cord were seated at a table on the restaurant patio that overlooked the local marina. The setting sun glittering off the water as boats moved in and out of the marina. After they placed their drink orders, Moira studied the menu. The place was a quaint French fusion restaurant. She quickly decided on what she wanted, closed her menu, sat it aside and studied Cord as he read his. The fading light cast delicious shadows across his features. Cupping her chin, she let her mind drift. If they managed to make this work between them, where would they be say five years from now?

She could easily see them living together. Having fun together. Her still writing, Cord running his bars. Sometimes she would see them living in Manhattan, others them in DC. She looked out over the water and sighed happily. If someone had told her that she would be this happy and content a year ago, she would have told them that was bollocks and to go hang themselves. A year ago, she had been pretty sure she would never find the type of happiness that her parents had, that she wrote about. Now, here on this beautiful tropical island she had hope that maybe, just maybe she had found that happiness.

***

Cord

Cord glanced over the top of his menu and watched Moira in the fading sunlight. The rays reflecting off her hair, making her look even more beautiful. She seemed to be deep in thought, at the moment and didn't notice when he closed his menu and sat it atop hers. Before he could speak, the waiter returned. He and Moira quickly gave their orders and they were once more alone. Cord reached out and took her hand.

"You seemed deep in thought there."

"Aye, I was."

"Care to share?"

"Well, I was thinking about us. You know, wondering where we would be in the future. I know we have some things to still work out."

"Moira, if you're worried about the fact that we live in different cities, we can and will figure that part out. Besides, DC and New York aren't that far away so we can come up with a solution you know." Cord said, stroking the back of her hand with his thumb.

"I know. I've only had one long distance relationship. My boyfriend in high school. I went to NYU he went to UCLA. Needless to say, things didn't end well. I think you and I have a much, much better chance." Moira explained, smiling.

Cord lifted her hand and kissed it. "So, you told Roxi about us and I told Collen. What about our parents?"

"I am very close with my parents Cord..."

"Baby, so am I. All I'm wondering is, will you be telling them when you get home or before? I want to tell my folks too, but I kind of want to tell them around the time you tell yours."

"When I get back, I think. I told Roxi I wanted to tell them today, but then I told her I'd rather wait till I got back. Face-to-face you know. I know my Da said that my brother Sean and his family were coming to dinner the Sunday after I get back. So, maybe then?" she questioned.

"Alright then. After you tell your family, you can either call or text me. I can then tell my parents. See, we can figure this out baby." He responded.

"Do your parents still live in North Carolina?"

"Yep in the same house me and Collen grew up in. I keep trying to talk them into getting a place closer to me and Collen, but they won't. Me and Collen have talked about building them a little cabin on some land me and Collen own in the country about two hours from Manhattan. That way, they have a place of their own near us."

"I think that's so sweet." Moira smiled.

Cord returned her smile. He glanced over as their food was being delivered. As he and Moira began eating, Cord's mind started wandering as hers had earlier. He could so vividly picture them and their families getting together for holidays and vacations. He and Moira in DC and Manhattan, living together, traveling together. His heart tripped at the thought of waking up every morning and going to bed every night with this amazing woman in his arms and in his bed. He vowed then and there he would fight to make that a reality.

CHAPTER ELEVEN

Cord

Three more days. That was how much longer he and Moira had together in paradise before they both returned to their lives and the real world. He looked up as Moira walked out of the bedroom. He felt himself smile as he drank her in. She was dressed in a blue button up short sleeve shirt over a lighter blue tank top. Short denim shorts hugged her hips and ass and the look was topped off with a pair of hiking boots. That fiery hair he loved was pulled up in a high ponytail. She looked delicious and he just wanted to take her back into her bedroom and throw her onto the bed.

"You look good." He commented.

"Thanks. Since we're going hiking again, I figured I might as well dress comfy." She grinned.

Last night Moira had pulled out Roxi's list and there were only two things left to do. One was a hike and the other was snorkeling. They would be doing that tomorrow and he was looking forward to it. Anything to see her in that bikini of hers he was completely on board with. The hike they were doing today wasn't a very long one, nor near as strenuous as the other three they had been on.

"Have you been on this hike before? Roxi said it may be short, but it's a beautiful one."

"Yeah it is. Of course, it's been a while since it's been several years since I've been here, but I do remember it. You'll like it."

Moira moved to him after she slipped on her day pack. Cord pulled her closer and kissed her sweetly. With their arms around each other, they exited Moira's condo and headed for the bus that would take them to the far side of the island for their hike. As they rode along, Cord told her what Collen had told him about the reopening of the bar. According to Collen, the reopening had been a huge success. Collen had even managed to score a band that was growing in popularity around NYU and Columbia.

"Sounds like your brother knows his stuff." Moira said.

"Yeah, Collie knows just as much about our business as I do, sometimes more. I've often asked him why he wants to stay in the background, but he just laughs and says he's the wizard behind the curtain." Cord chuckled.

It was an hour later, when the bus stopped at their destination, Cord helped Moira off the bus. They joined a group of tourists who also were going on the hike. Unlike the other tourists, Cord and Moira would not be making use of the guides. Cord had commented on the ride to their first hike at Pigeon National Park, that since they both were experienced hikers, what was the point of using a guide and Moira had agreed.

"You looking forward to going home?" he asked as they started down the trail.

"Yes and no." She answered. "I mean, like most people who go on vacation, you always look forward to going home at the end of it. I'm not because it means I won't be seeing you every day."

Cord heard the sadness that laced her voice. "I know what you mean. I've gotten spoiled by seeing you every day and used to having you in my arms at night."

"What are we going to do Cord? You're in Manhattan and I'm in DC..."

"Baby, we'll figure it all out. I promise. After you talk to your folks and I talk to mine, we'll come up with something."

***

Moira

It was midafternoon when she and Cord returned to the village. They climbed off the bus and made a beeline for the restaurant where they both had spotted each other the first day on the island. It was still the lunch rush, but she and Cord were able to find an empty table. After placing their orders, Cord reached out and took hold of her hand. Moira couldn't stop the smile and squeezed his hand.

"How's the new story coming along?" he inquired.

"I'm about half-way through it. If things keep on this track, I think I can have it finished and off to my editor by August. I texted my editor last week and told her about it and she's excited to read it." She replied.

"I can't wait to read it myself. From what little you've told me about it, it sounds good. Of course, my mom will rush out and buy it the day it hits bookstores. After she read your first book, she always picks up any book you release the day it comes out. My dad always grumbles about mom having too many books, but he doesn't mean it. In fact, for their anniversary this year he's having a custom build bookcase made for her. Me and Collen know about it because it's going to be delivered and installed while mom will be visiting us in New York."

"That's sweet. When is your ma coming out?"

"Their anniversary is June eighteenth. Mom is staying the week before."

Their food was delivered pausing their conversation. "And she doesn't suspect anything?"

Cord shook his head as he chewed his first bite. "Nope. Mom is an English teacher and dad is an architect. That's how grandpa made the family fortune, designing and building. We have six locations around North Carolina. Dad told mom he had a big project that week and couldn't get away."

Moira giggled, "Well, he does just for your ma. Did he design the bookcase?"

"Yep. It's a huge one too. It will take up the entire wall of mom's office. Me and Collen will be going back with mom after her week visit so we can be there for the unveiling. I asked dad how he's going to keep mom out of her office and he said he would call her two days before we go home and tell her that he's going to be redoing the carpet in there for her."

"Another half-truth?" she teased.

"Nope, he will replace the carpet then install the bookcase. Mom had been after him for new carpet in both their offices so he's taking the chance to do that and the bookcase while she's visiting."

Moira found herself really wanting to meet his parents. From the way Cord talked about them, she suspected they would be much like her own parents. Smart, successful, yet kind and caring people. A hint of nerves settled over her as she imagined Cord meeting her own parents. She liked to think her parents would like Cord, but when it came to introducing her boyfriend to her parents one could never be too sure how that would go. When she had introduced Phillip, her parents weren't too thrilled to meet him. Looking back, they saw what she hadn't. Phillip wasn't the right man for her.

"You alright? You seem a million miles away Moira."

Moira sighed, "Just wondering how things will go when and if we introduce each other to our parents."

Cord squeezed her hand, "Moira, my folks and Collen will love you. What's not to love? You're smart, funny, talented, and sweet to everyone around you. Not to mention, my mom is a huge fan so that alone will guarantee she will like you." Cord then frowned a little, "You're more worried about me meeting your parents, aren't you?"

Moira nodded and let out a breath, "I can't help it. When I introduced them to Phillip it didn't go very well. See, they somehow managed to see what I couldn't. That Phillip wasn't the good guy he tried to portray to everyone."

"Baby, I want to meet your folks. I want to meet the two people who brought you into this world. I want to tell them what an amazing woman you are and thank them for it, because of them, I was able to meet you."

Moira felt her eyes water at his words. Was this really happening? Had she finally met her perfect match that her mom said she would one day? His words dashed any fears she had of him meeting her family. Now, she was looking forward to going home and on Sunday she would happily tell her family about Cord. Then somehow, they would work out a way to get together so he could meet at least her parents. Maybe she could take them to New York for the day or even the weekend.

***

Cord

Cord held Moira to his side as they walked along the stretch of beach between their condos. After lunch, they went back to her place. He had made love to her in the shower then they curled up in each other's arms for a nap. Moira had surprised him and cooked a delicious dinner for them. As Cord had watched her cook, his heart fell even more under her spell. She wasn't just a smart pretty face. Moira Donovan was also one hell of a cook to boot. Since she had cooked, Cord had volunteered to do the dishes. Now, they were enjoying a moonlit walk. The soft lull of the water washing up over the sand and the floral scented breeze was the perfect backdrop.

"Moira, how about you come out to see me when my mom is in town? I mean, we're both going to tell them about us this weekend, right?" Cord suggested.

Moria stopped and faced him, "You mean it?"

"Hell, yeah I do. You could even bring your parents if you want. I mean if they can. You said your dad was a cop and your mom is a nurse. What do you say?" he nodded, wrapping his arms around her pulling her flush against him.

"I say, after I talk to them on Sunday, I'll let you know. If they can't make it, I'll still go. I love you Cord." She smiled.

Cord leaned down and kissed her. When he felt her body surrendering more into him, he slid his hands down and cupped her ass. He hoisted her up in his arms and moaned when her legs wrapped around his waist. His erection throbbed against her. Moira whimpered and began moving against him. Christ, he wanted this woman. Wanted to be buried inside her. He pulled away from her lips and looked around. He found they were right in front of his condo.

"I want you Moira. Fuck, I want you right now." He growled, moving toward his patio door.

"I want you too Cord. Please." She gasped, moving her lips against his neck.

Cord stumbled a little as her tongue started gliding along the pounding pulse point of his throat. Fumbling with his key, he managed to unlock the door and moved inside, barely managing to kick the door closed. His fingers tangled in Moira's hair, dragging her head back and capturing her lips once more. He navigated the dark condo and in moments they were in the bedroom. Deciding against turning on the light, Cord walked to the bed and lay her on it. The full moon shown through the windows, the moonbeams illuminating Moira.

"Moira...I want you naked. Right fucking now." Cord hissed, yanking off his shirt.

Moira smiled sitting up. As Cord stripped, he watched his woman strip for him. First to go was her purple halter top. The soft moonlight shimmered on the pale skin of her breasts. God, he loved her tits. Her hardening nipples a soft rosy color and just begging for his mouth. He stepped out of his shorts and boxers as Moira lay back, lifting her hips and shoving down her own shorts. Cord cursed when he saw she had been completely commando.

"God almighty, you were cooking dinner with nothing on but your shorts and shirt?" he groaned, kneeling on the bed.

"Aye I was." She smirked.

Cord moved over her. He gripped her calves and locking her legs around him. "Damn, you're wet."

"All it seems to take is one kiss and that look in your eyes and I'm wet for you Cord." She sighed, her back bowing.

Elevating her hips, Cord eased himself inside her. Moira gasped his name and Cord could only moan. Cord set a slow pace. When he brought her inside, he had been wild, but now that they were naked and he was inside her, he wanted to take his time. After tonight, they only had two more days together. They were going back home on Friday, sadly on separate flights. She was leaving at nine in the morning and he wasn't flying out till eleven. He wanted to make their last days count.

"You feel so good Moira. Like you're made for me."

"Aye, you fit me perfectly."

Cord shifted their positions and blanketed her body with his. Every thrust was met with her body arching and welcoming him deeper each time. Her legs anchoring their hips together, her nails slowly and sensually scraping along his back and shoulders. No woman had ever made him feel like this. Wild and centered, blind with need and yet able to see more clearly than ever. It was perfect. Moira Donovan was perfect. And she was his.

CHAPTER TWELVE

Moira

Moira exited the plane and found her mom and dad waiting for her. She hurried over and was swept up in a double hug from them. "Hi ma, hi da."

"Oh, welcome home m'iníon." Kiernan said.

"You look like you had a good trip." Maureen added.

"I did. It was so beautiful there. You two should go after you retire." Moira grinned.

With her in-between her parents and her arms around their waists, the three moved from the gate toward baggage claim. After collecting her bags, they walked out to her parent's car. On the drive to Moira's house from Reagan National, Moira told them about her trip to St. Lucia. Excluding Cord, but only slightly. She did tell them she met someone, but not that she and Cord were a couple. She would drop that bombshell on Sunday when Sean and Laura would be there. Her thought was, if she was going to tell her parents she might as well tell the rest of the family.

"Are you happy to be home?" Maureen asked.

"Aye ma, I'm very happy. I had fun, but it's always good to be home." Moira answered.

"Aye, that's very true." Kiernan agreed.

About half an hour later, Moira and her parents were in her apartment. As Moira and Maureen headed into the bedroom, Kiernan set about making them all some coffee. Silently, Maureen and Moira started unpacking her two suitcases. Moira found herself starting to say something to her mother about Cord but stopped herself at the last minute. No, she would wait till Sunday dinner at her childhood home before she brought up Cord O'Brien.

"I hope you took pictures." Maureen stated, dropping a pile of shirts in the hamper.

"Oh, aye I did, and no not on just my phone. I finally got the chance to use that camera Laura gave me last year." Moira grinned. The pictures on her phone were mostly of her and Cord anyway.

"I hope you will bring it on Sunday and show us all of them." Maureen said.

"Of course." Moira nodded, as she dropped the last of her vacation clothes in the hamper.

She and her mom tucked the suitcases into the hall closet and the two women walked into the kitchen where Kiernan had just finished fixing them their coffee. Over coffee, Moira filled her parents in about her trip, again, not quite telling them everything about Cord. When she told her mom about the recipe she had gotten from Amelia, Maureen insisted on getting a copy to make it for Sunday dinner.

"Well, yer ma and I are heading home. You just relax and we'll see you on Sunday." Kiernan said, rising from his chair then helping Maureen to her feet.

"We're glad you're home." Maureen replied, hugging Moira.

"I'm glad to be home too ma. I'll see you on Sunday."

Moira walked her parents to the door and stood there as they climbed back into the car. She waved as they backed out and drove off. Sighing, Moira reentered the apartment. She headed into her bedroom, grabbed a change of clothes, and took a relaxing shower. Fresh and clean again, Moria moved into her living room and clicked on the tv.

***

Cord

"Collie!" Cord called out, spotting his brother at the gate.

"Welcome back." Collen laughed.

Cord hugged his younger brother. "It's good to be home. So, fill me in on how things are going."

"Things are going fine. The bars are starting to get a bit busier now that school is out. We hired a new bartender at the Bronx location. Her name is Joanie. We also took on a few new waitresses at the Manhattan bar." Collen began.

Cord frowned, "Why does that name sound familiar?"

"Probably because she and I were friends back in school."

"Wait, THAT Joanie? The one that tutored you in psych?"

"The same one. She applied and out of the four others she was best. Wait till you see for yourself, she's freakin' awesome and the other staff there like her."

"Do you know when she's working again?"

Collen pulled out his phone as Cord picked up his bags. "Looks like she's working tomorrow night."

"Then I'll swing by tomorrow night and reintroduce myself and check her out. Course, if you say she's good that means she is." Cord nodded, falling into step with Collen as they headed for the parking garage.

Once in Collen's truck, Cord pulled out his own phone and turned it back on. He found a text from Moira letting him know she was back home safe and sound and relaxing. Cord would call her in a little bit after he got home, unpacked, and showered off the travel. After shooting off a text to Moira letting her know he was back, he caught a smirk on Collen's face. "What?"

"Nothing." Collen chuckled.

"Spit it out Collie." Cord pushed.

"Fine, I was just thinking it's kinda funny seeing you grinning like an idiot. I'm guessing you were texting Moira."

Cord sighed, "Yes. I don't know what it is about her, but from the moment I met Moira it was like bam! We just clicked Collen."

"Hey, I'm not teasing. I think it's great. It's obvious how you talked about her last week and seeing you now that she makes you happy, then she's got major points with me. You're my big brother and I just want to see you happy." Collen stated. "When am I going to meet her?"

"Actually, I suggested she and her folks, if they can, come out when mom's here. On Sunday she's telling her family about us and after she tells me how that goes, I'll be calling up mom and dad and doing the same." Cord answered.

"Sounds good. It's been killing me not telling mom and dad. But you better tell them that you swore me to secrecy or I'm gonna kick your ass." Collen threatened.

"I will." Cord laughed.

***

Moira

Moira took a slow breath before she walked into her childhood home. Already she could hear her two nephews running through the house with Sean yelling at them to stop running. They were the first to see her. "Aunt Moira!"

"Hey Brian, Lucas." Moira grinned, gathering the boys in a tight hug. "Giving yer da a hard time I see."

"They bloody well are." Sean grumbled, stepping into the entryway. He pulled Moira into a hug after she released the boys. "Welcome home deirfiúr bheag."

Moira chuckled at Sean using Irish to call her little sister. "Thanks. And thank you again for the trip."

"Me and Laura, along with ma and da were happy to do it. You deserved it after the last year." Sean shrugged. Ma and Laura are in the kitchen and da is watching the Yankees play."

Moira nodded. She and Sean walked into the living room where Kiernan was yelling at the umpire for a bad call. Chuckling, Moira dropped a kiss on his cheek and left her da, brother and nephews to their game. Walking into the kitchen, she found Maureen and her sister-in-law working on dinner. Laura spotted Moira first and moved over to hug her tightly. Moira had loved Laura from day one and the two women were as close as she and Sean were.

"Mom told me you had a good time." Laura said.

"Aye, I had a blast. Thank you for the trip. I already told ma and da they need to go next year after they retire." Moira replied, slipping into a bar stool at the island.

"That's what Sean and I said too." Laura smiled.

"Will ye three let your Da and I ACTUALLY retire first." Maureen complained good naturedly, causing Moira and Laura to laugh.

As Maureen and Laura finished up the stew, Moira sat there just keeping them company. Occasionally a yell would filter in from the living room causing Maureen and Laura to roll their eyes and Moira would giggle. Maureen and Laura didn't follow sports of any kind too much, but Moira enjoyed baseball. Unlike her Da and brother however, she didn't have a favorite team. Her Da was also a fan of football and soccer. When he was asked why soccer he would always say, *"I'm Irish aren't I?"*

Half an hour later everyone was seated at the table. Moira fidgeted as she ate. She wanted to say something before they started eating but figured her Da and brother would take the news better if they had full bellies. She knew her mom and Laura would be on her side so long as she was happy, but Kiernan and Sean were always protective of her when it came to dating. Even now despite Moira being thirty-two years old. Dinner at the Donovan house was a lively affair. Brian and Lucas were filling Moira in on their last few weeks of school. Laura, who was a teacher, expressed her relief that another school year was finished.

"Don't get me wrong, I love being a teacher, but sometimes high school kids can be a bit of a handful." Laura chuckled.

"I'd never have the patience to be a teacher." Moira grinned.

"I'm with Moira. I have a bloody hard time training grown men." Sean added.

After Sean had left the Marines and he and Laura moved to Norfolk, he joined the Norfolk police department. Last year he had been promoted to instructor at the police academy. He loved it and the hours were more convenient with having two younger boys. Brian and Lucas were going into second and fourth. Sean said once both were in middle school, he might try for the Detective's test and see what happened after that. Moira noticed that everyone seemed to be finished eating and decided now was the time.

"Um, I have something I want to tell all of ye." Moira spoke up.

Maureen took one look at her daughter and turned to her grandsons. "Brian, Lucas, why donna you two go out back and play."

"Yes grandma." The boys answered, hopping up from the table and running outside.

Moira took a slow breath, "While I was in St. Lucia, I...well...I met someone."

Kiernan's eyes narrowed slightly, "You met someone?"

"Aye Da. We met that first day. His name is Cord O'Brien. He and his brother Collen own and run seven bars in and around New York City."

"He owns bars. Moira, you canna be serious." Sean jumped in.

"Sean, Cord is a good man. He and I have a lot in common. He's a complete gentleman. Cord is smart, funny, and not that it matters, he's wealthy. His bars,

O'Brien's Tap, are remarkably successful. His ma is a teacher and his da is an architect." Moira added

"He sounds like a nice young man." Maureen said.

"Oh, he is ma. He's so sweet and he's read my books. He says his ma is a huge fan and she got him to read my stuff. Cord says he's read my suspense stuff but not my pure romance stuff." Moira nodded.

"You sound like you're in love." Laura laughed.

"I am Laura. Cord said he loved me first." Moira replied.

"Moira, but you two only knew each other what, three weeks?" Kiernan argued.

Moira sighed, "Da, I know it's only been a short time, but I know what I'm feeling. Cord and I just fit. I know he lives in New York and I'm here, but we can figure it out. In fact, next month his ma is coming out for a visit. His da is working on an anniversary surprise and is using this visit to do it. Cord wants me to come up to meet her. He also said to bring you and ma as well. Hell, even Sean and Laura if they could but he understands if you can't because you live in Norfolk."

Silence fell over the table. Moira could see that Laura and Maureen were happy for her and fully supportive. Sean and Kiernan however looked to be having doubts. Moira could see where they would be having them. Yet, she also knew her own heart and mind. She loved Cord and knew he loved her. Moira looked from her brother and father waiting for one of them to speak up. It was Sean.

"Moira, you're my deirfiúr bheag and you always will be. But, if you're sure about how you feel toward this O'Brien guy then I'm happy for you." Sean sighed.

"I'm completely sure Sean. Just wait, once you meet him, you'll see for yourself." Moira smiled.

Kiernan let out a low breath, "Well, I suppose yer ma and I could go with you to meet his ma. Just let me know the dates and I'll see what I can do."

Moira hopped up from her chair and hurried over to her Da and hugged him, "Oh thank you Da."

***

Cord

Cord waited for his mom or dad to answer. Ten minutes ago, Moira had texted him telling him how her family had taken the news. She also said her mom and dad would be coming out to New York to meet his mom. Now, Cord was the one feeling nervous about telling his parents about Moira. He took a few slow breaths when his mother answered the phone. *"Hello?"*

"Hey mom."

"Oh Cord, you're home. How was your trip? I hope you actually relaxed." Sally O'Brien teased.

"I did mom. In fact, well, is dad there?" Cord asked.

"He's right here. Do you want me to put this on speaker phone? " Sally questioned.

"Yeah, that would be easier since I have something to tell you both."

There was silence for a few moments before Cord heard his dad, *"Hello Cord."* Peter O'Brien greeted.

"Hi pop. Well, while I was in St. Lucia, I met someone." Cord began.

For the next few minutes, Cord told his parents about his time with Moira. He told them how they met and how much fun they had together. As expected, when he revealed who Moira was, his mom was beyond excited. That took a few moments to calm her so Cord could continue and caused Peter to just laugh at his wife's antics. When he dropped the bombshell that he and Moira were in love, there was nothing but silence from his parents.

"Mom? Dad? You still there?" Cord asked.

"We're here. Cord, are you sure? I mean, you've never even shown any interest in being a one-woman man." Sally replied.

"Jeez mom, you make me sound like a gigolo." Cord groaned.

"That's not what your mom is saying." Peter chuckled, *"But you have to admit, it seems a bit out of the blue for you. You used to say you weren't ready to settle down."*

Cord sighed, "I know but then...hell, I don't know. When I met Moira and we started spending time together, it just felt so right. I know we haven't known each other long, but I know I love her, and she loves me. I even asked her to come to New York next month to meet mom and to bring her folks if they can."

"Oh, I'd love that. And not just because I'm a fan. I want to meet the woman who has won your heart." Sally gushed.

"Cord, you've always used sound judgment and you're not one to just jump in blind. If you say you love her then of course I will support, you. Since I can't come out with your mother, I'll just have to find time soon to go out myself and meet her." Peter said.

"I promise, once you meet her, you two will love her. Oh, I need to say that Collen knew. I told him first and I swore him to secrecy. He had called and I was bursting to tell someone, and he just happened to be that person. I wanted to be the one to tell you and he wasn't happy about keeping this from you guys." Cord stated.

"Then we won't be mad at Collen. At least you didn't wait too long to tell us." Sally teased.

Cord and his parents talked a little longer before he hung up. After that call, he texted Moira to let her know how things went. She sent him a laughing face emoji when he told her about his mom practically squealing when he told her that he was now dating her favorite author. Cord also told her that his mom was looking forward to meeting her and her parents. When Cord and Moira finally said goodnight, he felt relieved. Soon the woman he loved would meet his family and he would meet hers. He couldn't wait.

CHAPTER THIRTEEN

Moira

Moira was nervous as she and her parents walked up to the restaurant where they would be meeting Cord, Collen, and Sally. For the last two weeks, Moira had tried to calm her nerves. Cord had told her that it would be fine and to just be herself. Yeah, that was easier said than done, as far as Moira was concerned. Cord had surprised her yet again when he called up her parents a week after she had told them about him. When Moira found out she was floored. Kiernan had told her, and he said that he appreciated Cord doing that and whatever the two men had talked about, it had shifted Kiernan Donovan's view and he was more supportive about this.

"You seem nervous Moira." Maureen teased just before they walked in.

"I am ma. I don't know why but I am." Moira admitted.

"Everything will be fine. You'll see." Kiernan added, holding open the door for his wife and daughter.

Moira hoped so. She walked in first and started scanning the room. Before the Host could ask how many, she spotted Cord making his way toward them. Christ the man looked even more handsome now than he had when they parted at the airport in St. Lucia nearly three weeks ago. When Cord reached them, he immediately gathered Moira into his arms and kissed her tenderly. The kiss was short, but still lit Moira's blood on fire. Cord released her lips and keeping her tucked into his side, faced her parents.

"Mr. and Mrs. Donovan, It's nice to finally meet you both. I'm Cord." Cord said, extending his hand.

Kiernan was the first to take it, "It's nice to meet ya too Cord. Please, call me Kiernan."

"I'm Maureen. You are just as my Moira described." Maureen greeted, taking Cord's hand.

"As are you. Well, shall we? My mom and brother are waiting." Cord smiled.

Moira let out a slow breath. She felt less nervous with Cord's arm wrapped around her. When they rounded a slight corner, she found a table waiting. The young man who stood looked a lot like Cord. There was no mistaking that the two were related. Collen walked over and in a move that surprised Moira, he hugged her then kissed her cheek. "I'm Collen. I guess you're the one I have to thank for putting the smile on my big brother's face?"

Moira giggled, "I suppose so."

As Collen introduced himself to her parents, Moira turned and faced the woman who just rose from the table. Cord held her hand and moved them toward her. "Moira, this is my mom, Sally O'Brien. Mom, I'd like you to meet Moira Donovan."

"Oh, I'm so happy to meet you honey." Sally beamed as she too hugged Moira.

Moira returned the hug feeling the last of her nerves vanish in a blink. "It's so nice to meet ye too Mrs. O'Brien."

"Please call me Sally. You say Mrs. O'Brien and I'm either looking for my mother-in-law or one of my students." Sally chuckled. "Are these your parents?"

"Aye. Ma, Da, this is Cord's mother, Sally. Sally, this is my ma and da, Maureen and Kiernan." Moira introduced.

***

Cord

Cord sat between Moira and her mother. All through the meal, the six of them talked about anything and everything it seemed. His mom, of course, had to gush over Moira's books and Moira, the wonder that she was, presented Sally with an autographed copy of her latest release. Collen and Kiernan were in deep discussion about the current roster for the Yankees and the upcoming football season. Cord looked over when Moira squeezed his hand.

"You okay baby?" he asked.

"Aye, I am now. I was nervous when we first got here, I'll admit." She answered.

Cord leaned over and kissed her forehead, "I told you there was no reason to be. Seems our moms are getting along, and Collen has found a fellow sports enthusiast in your dad."

"It seems that way." Moira giggled.

"So, are you three in town for the weekend or just for the afternoon?" Cord asked Maureen and Kiernan.

"Sadly, Maureen and I could only get the day. We'll be driving back to DC after lunch." Kiernan answered.

"I drove up with ma and da." Moira added, a little sadly.

"I know how it can be not being able to get time off work. My husband Peter had to stay in North Carolina because he has a big project that he couldn't leave at the moment." Sally said, missing the knowing looks her sons shared.

"Well, then we will have to find some time for us to stay longer next time." Maureen replied with a smile.

Cord hid his disappointment about Moira not being able to stay at least the night. His mom was staying with Collen since Collen didn't work near as long hours as Cord did. Course, Cord would visit all the bars throughout the city just to make sure everything was running smoothly. Yet he was still happy that at least for the afternoon with Moira and finally he met her parents. Already he was thinking of maybe surprising her by driving out to DC the day after his mom left.

After lunch, Cord and his family walked with Moira and hers to where they had parked a few blocks away. Maureen and Sally were in conversation as were Collen and Kiernan, leaving Cord and Moira to follow holding hands. "I'm glad I finally got to meet your parents Moira. They seem like great people."

"Aye, I could say the same about your ma and brother. I'm actually looking forward to in the future getting our families together again." Moira smiled.

Cord leaned over and kissed the top of her head. The group reached the Donovan's car and began saying their goodbyes. When Moira went to say bye to his mom, Cord had to smile when Sally pulled Moira into her arms for a tight hug. He enjoyed seeing the big, bright smile that the hug caused to appear on Moira's face. It warmed his heart to see that his family had accepted her. Then it was his turn to be surprised when Maureen pulled him into a fierce hug.

"It was nice to meet you Cord. I hope we see you soon." Maureen stated.

"Believe me Maureen, I plan to stick around as long as Moira will have me." Cord nodded.

Kiernan stepped up and shook Cord's hand, "You seem to make me daughter happy. For that, thank you."

"It's my pleasure. For the record sir, your daughter makes me happy as well." Cord replied.

Moira and Cord shared a soft kiss goodbye before she slipped into the backseat. As the car pulled out into the evening flow of traffic, a sadness fell over Cord. He turned to look when he sensed his mom next to him. "Well mama, what do you think?"

"I think she's a terrific young lady and a good fit for you. I hope to see more of her and of her parents." Sally smiled.

"Me too mama, me too." Cord agreed.

***

Moira

Moira sighed stepping out the bathroom. The day had been fun. She liked Cord's mom and brother and it seemed that now that her parents had met Cord, they liked him too. She had managed to hide her disappointment about not being able to stay longer than the afternoon, but at least she got to see him. Pulling the wrapped towel from her head, she began drying her hair as she headed for the bed. She had just sat down when her phone rang. She grinned when she saw it was Cord.

"Hi."

"Hey there. It was so good seeing you today. And meeting your folks. I liked them. Collen was in awe of your dad I think."

"Aye, me da liked Collen. So, tell him the feeling is mutual. Me ma adored yours. The whole drive back both ma and da kept saying how much they enjoyed today and getting to meet you, Collen and Sally."

"Mom was over the moon when you gave her that autographed book. She says the second she gets home she's putting it in a special place." Cord laughed.

"Well, when she gets home, she'll have a brand-new bookcase waiting for her." Moira giggled. "After meeting your ma and brother, I can't wait to meet your da."

"You'll love pop. And just like mom, he'll adore you too. I hope soon I get to meet your brother, sister-in-law, and nephews. Maybe you and I could drive down there for a weekend or something."

"I'd love that. I could drive to New York then we could head out together. I really wish I could have stayed at least the night, but I figured your ma was staying with you, that's why I rode with ma and da."

"No, when mom and dad come to visit, they stay with Collen. I tend to work longer hours. I'm the face of the bars so I try to visit all seven during the week and weekend. Collen handles the behind the scenes stuff. He books the bands, does the advertising, but we both tackle the payroll and stuff."

Moira shifted so that she was laying on the bed, pillows propped up against the headboard. "So, what are you doing now?"

"Just sitting on my sofa, wishing you were here. What about you?"

"I had just got out of the shower. I'm on my bed right now in just a robe." She heard Cord let out one of those deep growls that drove her wild. "Now I'm really wishing I was there with you."

"Me too. I love seeing you fresh from the shower. Your hair wet and wild. Your body flushed from the heat. Your skin so soft and extremely sensitive."

Moira whimpered as her body began reacting to his words. "I miss you."

"I miss you too baby. God, I wanted you so bad when I saw you today. I wanted to just grab you, carry you off to my place and take you straight to my bed."

"I felt the same. Seeing you today had me wanting you just as bad."

"Moira, touch yourself for me."

***

Cord

Cord heard Moira's breath hitch at his request. "Please baby. You don't need to speak, just listen to my words. Imagine your hand is mine. I want you to tease that amazing body of yours for me."

He felt his erection throb when Moira gasped his name. *"Cord. Bloody hell, my nipples are so hard."*

"That's right Moira. Tease them. Pinch them. Your fingers are my mouth. Tasting you. Nipping those hard nipples." Cord breathed, reaching down to adjust himself. "You're getting hot aren't you baby? Hot and wet for me. Your legs parting. Wanting more."

"Yes. Please."

"If I was there, I'd already be touching that sweet pussy of yours. Feeling how wet I make you. Slipping a finger, then two, inside you. Making your buck into my hand." Cord couldn't stand it. He quickly pulled himself free of his boxers as he heard Moira gasping. "You're touching that pussy, aren't you?"

"Y...yes..."

"Nice and slow baby. Make yourself wetter for me. God, I'm hard as stone here."

"You're...stroking..."

"Yes. I couldn't help it. Now, move those fingers faster Moira. Faster. Deeper." He ordered as his own hand started moving faster. "I'm deep inside you now. Taking you. Just the way you like it."

Cord moaned as Moira's gasps and whimpers filled his ears. In his mind he could picture her. Laying on her bed, that robe opened. Her legs spread wide as her fingers slid inside her deeper and deeper with each thrust. Her back bowing as it did whenever he hit the right spot. He squeezed his cock tighter when his name echoed from the phone. She was getting closer and by god, so was he.

"Faster baby. Ride your fingers, picture my cock deep inside you. You're close, aren't you?"

"Yes...close...oh Cord. Please." Moira pleaded.

"That's it. Ride my cock Moira. Harder. Faster. I want you to explode for me. I'm so close baby." Cord groaned, his hand jerking faster.

Just as he felt his climax hit, Moira all but screamed his name. That was the last straw and he exploded with her, calling her name as his orgasm rocked through him. For several long minutes, the only sounds were his and Moira's ragged breathing. He moaned a little as he shifted on his couch. He smiled when he heard Moira starting to giggle.

"Oh my God. I have to say that was a first for me."

"What do you mean?" he asked.

"I've written a few phone sex scenes in my books, but I've never actually done it. Wow, that was hot." She replied.

"I'll say it was. And for the record, I've never had phone sex either. Guess we found a new way to get each other off when we can't physically be together."

"Aye. I think I'm already looking forward to us doing this again."

"Me too." He smiled. "Well, I better go. Collen and I are taking mom to breakfast and sightseeing in the morning. I love you Moira."

"I love you too Cord. Good night."

Cord waited till she hung up before he did. He got to his feet and headed for the bathroom to clean up. After washing up and changing his boxers, he returned to the living room to clean up the hot mess he made. As he climbed into bed, he made his mind up that he would definitely be making a drive to DC after he and Collen put his mom on the plane. Yes, he loved his mom, but he wanted to spend more than a few hours with Moira.

CHAPTER FOURTEEN

Moira

Moira typed away furiously. Once she got home and settled again from her three-week trip, she had started back to work. Her editor Holly had gone through nearly half of the novel Moira had sent to her before going on vacation. Now the work really began. Moira was one of the few authors she knew that didn't mind editing. From the very beginning, Moira had insisted that her editor shred her story. Moira believed that a writer couldn't get better at their craft if the editors' sugar-coated things. How was a writer to know what needed work if they first didn't know what the problem was?

Holly was Moira's favorite editor and for the last three years or so the two worked exclusively together. The pair had a great work relationship as well as a personal one. Whenever Moira went to meet with her publishers in New York, which usually was a weeklong trip, she would stay with Holly. However, with Cord in her life now, that would probably change. Moira had yet to let Holly know about him but planned to do so once she finished her current edits. Or that had been the plan till her phone rang and she saw it was Holly.

"Hey Holly."

"Hey there. I'm assuming you received the first group of edits." Holly began.

"Aye, I'm working on them now. I will say, it's funny you called."

"Oh?"

Moira wasted no time in filling Holly in about meeting Cord in St. Lucia. She told her friend about how they were now dating and while yes, they lived in separate cities, they were working on figuring that logistic out. Moira also told her about meeting Cord's mom and brother and him meeting her parents. Holly listened intently and when Moira finished her tale, Holly squealed in delight for her.

"Oh, Moira that's great! This sounds like the perfect premise for one of your novels. Maybe you could talk to your man and see if he would be okay with you writing your story. Of course, you would want to change the names and such just to be safe." Holly suggested.

Moira laughed, "His ma Sally said the same thing. Seems she's a huge fan of mine and that's how Cord knew who I was when we met that first day. God Holly, he's amazing. He's funny, smart, and the most handsome man I've ever seen, let alone met."

"You said he and his brother own several bars here in New York? Which ones?"
"O'Brien's Tap."

"Well I'll be damned! When you finally hook up with a guy you go for the big fish don't you." Holly laughed. *"He and his brother were just in* The Voice *last week. Seems a city councilman's son had been a bit drunk and caused some damage at their Manhattan location. I believe it was Councilman Walker. Walker not only paid for the repairs, but made his son help. The press release stated that Walker used this latest incident to teach his son that just because he was the son of a wealthy councilman, didn't give him the right to behave like spoiled child."*

"Wow, I remember Cord telling me he was on vacation while some renovations were being done to one of the bars, but he didn't tell me that. Course, I didn't ask either."

"I've been to the one in Manhattan as well as the one in SoHo. They are great places to go and have fun and relax. At least twice a month they have live music on Friday and Saturday night. I got to see Jason Mraz once and let me tell you it was great."

"I bet." Moira smiled. Holly was a huge Jason Mraz fan. "So, whenever I make a trip to meet the publishers, unless Cord says differently, I'm assuming he's going to want me to stay with him."

"He'd be a fool not to want you to stay with him. So, you saw him last weekend with your parents? How did that go?" Holly chuckled.

"It went great. His mom and brother were so sweet and my Da and Collen spent most of the time talking sports. Ma and Sally talked about everything from books, to music, to movies. It honestly felt like we had known each other forever." Moira replied.

"That's great honey. Well, I'll let you get back to work. If it's alright, I can send the next group of edits to you."

"Send them away. I'm nearly done with this group."

"Will do. I'll talk to you later Moira."

Moira bid Holly goodbye and went back to work. As she worked, she thought over the idea of writing her and Cord's story. Of course, before she even started, she would first make sure he was okay with it. This wouldn't be like her previous work which was all fiction. This would be true events. She couldn't stop from smiling at the idea of writing it. She hoped Cord would be fine with it.

***

Cord

Cord sat at his desk looking over the floor plan of a building. After the previous weekend's successful meeting of his family and Moira's, an idea had hit. For the last week he had been combing over the financials and looking at several locations that looked promising. The one thing he hadn't done yet was fill Collen in on his plans. He was still debating it. Should he do it now? Should he wait? Should he even bring it up to Collen just yet? Cord sighed and closed the folder he had started for this idea. There was a knock on his door followed by Collen poking his head in.

"Hey there." Collen greeted.

"Hey Collie. What's up?" Cord asked, leaning back in his chair.

"Just thought you'd like to see the numbers from the past week." Collen stated, handing over a folder.

When Cord opened it and looked at them, he felt his eyes widen and his jaw drop. "Holy shit. This is from one week?"

"Yep, and that's for all SEVEN locations." Collen grinned.

Cord was floored. True their bars were popular, but in the last week their weekly revenue had nearly doubled. "What the hell caused this huge jump?"

"If I had to guess, I'd say that article in The Voice. Plus, Councilman Walker also talked to a few reporters afterward. Like he promised, he didn't sugar coat a damned thing regarding what happened with his kid. I took those numbers over to Al and his models all seem to indicate that we can see those numbers continuing to increase steadily over the next several months, maybe longer." Collen explained.

Al was their analysts' guy. He was also Collen's best friend. Al had been with the O'Brien brothers from the beginning. The guy was a whiz at projections.

He had been the one to determine the best location for their first bar which was the Bronx. Damned if he hadn't been right too. In fact, thanks to Al, they had made nearly a million their first year. "This is great. I think we owe Al not only a raise but a steak dinner."

"I agree. And if you're ready for an even bigger shock, I just got off the phone with the manager for Five Finger Death Punch. They want to do a small concert to promote their upcoming album at our Manhattan bar." Collen added.

"Fuck me. Really?" Cord gaped.

"Really. I told their manager I would talk to you and then call him back about dates and logistics. He did say it would be a private gig. They would sell passes for maybe 150 people. As the venue, we would receive twenty percent of ticket sales. He would also give us twenty free passes for us to sell or giveaway. If we choose to sell those, we get all the profits of those sales." Collen said.

"I say get your ass back in your office and call him and say hell yeah." Cord ordered.

Collen laughed, gave a two-finger salute and left. Cord couldn't believe this was happening. He glanced at his watch and jumped to his feet. He was late for meeting with his mom. He and her were having lunch today at her favorite place. Tucking the files Collen had given him in his desk, Cord rushed from his office. Luckily, he caught a cab and got to the restaurant only five minutes late.

"Hey mom, sorry I'm late." Cord apologized, kissing her cheek.

"I figured you got held up baby." Sally smiled.

"Mom, you're not going to believe what just happened." Cord replied and proceeded to tell her the good news.

***

Moira

Moira and Roxi were having lunch at their favorite bistro in Georgetown. "So, how's things going at work?" Moira asked.

"Things are going good. I'll be heading off to Cleveland next week to cover the campaign." Roxi answered.

Moira and Roxi had grown up in DC and from the age of twelve, Roxi had been interested in politics. She was now a political analyst for the Republican party. This election season she was assigned to a Republican Senator from Ohio. Unlike Roxi, Moira wasn't too interested in politics. Yet despite that, she and Roxi still had lots in common and still had a blast together. When Roxi had been hired just before they graduated college, Moira had been thrilled for her.

"That's great. Be sure you bring me back a neat souvenir." Moira teased.

"Don't I always." Roxi winked. "How's the editing going?"

"It's going good. I'm about halfway through the first round. Holly says at this rate, the books should be released about the second week of September. The publishing house is already working on the promotions and stuff."

"That's awesome girl. I can't wait to read it. It will give me something to take my mind off politics for a bit."

Moira laughed. While Roxi might sometimes complain about politics, the woman lived for the rush of it. "I'll be sure to get you a copy."

"Have you heard from Cord since last week?" Roxi questioned, changing gears.

"Actually, I have." Moira nodded, trying to hide the blush as she recalled the phone sex session, they had the night she met his mom and brother. But failed.

"You're blushing."

"Shut up, no I'm not."

"Okay, now you have to tell me. What happened, did you two have a phone sex session..." Roxi paused when Moira's blush deepened. "Oh my god! You did!"

As Roxi laughed, Moira covered her face with her hands. "Bloody hell, this is embarrassing."

"Why? Hell Moira, you write stuff like this in your books."

"Yes, I write it, but I've never actually done it." Moira argued.

"So now you have. It's not that big of a deal really." Roxi replied.

"Wait, you mean you've done that before?" Moira inquired.

"A few times yeah. It's kind of fun actually. Only having your partners voice and your imagination. It can be a nice form of foreplay." Roxi nodded, reaching for her tea.

"That's kinda what Cord said too afterward. I will admit, it was hot as hell." Moira admitted.

"I will say this, since you told me about Cord, you just seem and sound happier."

"I am Roxi. After what happened with Phillip, Cord is…God I don't know. He's the complete opposite. I've never dated anyone like him. It's like we just know each other."

Roxi cupped her chin, "And that is what it's all about. When I finally meet him, I'm warning you now, I'm giving him a big hug and a kiss for making my best friend happy."

Moira laughed, "Since you warned me, I'll allow it."

"Good." Roxi nodded firmly.

***

Cord

Cord flopped on his sofa. He was tired, but happy. After telling his mom at lunch about the good news from Collen she had been beyond thrilled for her sons. Collen had set up things for Five Finger Death Punch and the date was set for the third Friday in June. Cord still couldn't wrap his mind around this. True, O'Brien's Tap had been doing well the last ten years, but the information he received today was beyond anything he could imagine. After lunch with his mom, Cord had gone to see Al. With the information about the private gig in June, Al had re-crunched his numbers and they were even better than before. Cord groaned when he heard his phone ring.

"Yeah?"

"Did I call at a bad time?"

Cord smiled, "It's never a bad time when you call baby."

"You sound tired boyo." Moira teased.

"I am but in a good way. Hey, have you ever heard of Five Finger Death Punch?"

"Are you bloody kidding? I love them. Me and Roxi got to see them at the Garden a few years ago."

"How would you like to be my guest at a private gig they're doing at our Manhattan location the third Friday in June?"

"Seriously? Oh, Cord that's bloody terrific for you! I'd love to be your guest. My editor Holly said there was an article about you and Collen in The Voice last week."

"Yeah and thanks to that article, it seems business is on an upswing." Cord said. He then told her about the numbers Collen and Al had given him and the details of the gig in June.

"Oh Cord, this is wonderful. I'm so happy for you boyo." Moira beamed.

"I still can't believe this is really happening. But the best part about it is that I get to tell you about it. To share this with you. I love you so damned much Moira."

"And I love you too Cord. I'm honored that you want to share this with me. It makes this all the sweeter."

Cord and Moira talked a little longer, but she ended it telling him he needed to get some sleep. As much as he didn't want to, he knew she was right. After telling each other good night, it was Cord who hung up first. Somehow, he managed to get to his feet and grabbed a shower. He felt bone weary when he slipped between the sheets. Despite that, he had made a decision based on his idea. He would do a bit more research and if things still looked good, after the concert in June he would move forward with his plans.

CHAPTER FIFTEEN

Moira

Moira zipped up her bag, "Well, I think I have everything."

"You're grinning like a fool." Roxi teased from where she sat on Moira's bed.

"I can't help it." Moira sighed happily. "I'm spending a whole week with Cord. At his house. I know we spent most of our trip in St. Lucia together, but this is different. I mean, it feels different anyway."

Roxi nodded, "It is different honey. You're seeing him on his home turf. That would be daunting to most women."

Moira sat beside her best friend, "Roxi, do you think me; and Cord are crazy? I mean we've only known each other what...two months now and we said, 'I love you' to each other after only two weeks."

"Moira, that's not crazy. At least not to me. Look at my parents for example. They dated only three months then got married. I think THAT'S crazy." Roxi paused and studied Moira. "You and Cord aren't thinking of running off and getting married this week, are you?"

"What? No!" Moira laughed. "My ma and da would kill me if I did that. Ma has had me wedding planned since I was five, so I couldn't elope if I tried."

"True, your catholic guilt wouldn't let you." Roxi said thoughtfully.

"Oh, sod off." Moira huffed, making Roxi laugh. "I gotta go or I'm going to hit traffic. Will you lock up for me?"

"Sure. Once I finish my laundry I'll lock up. Now, you get going and have fun. If you meet the band, I want pictures and an autograph bitch."

Moira laughed as she hugged Roxi. Pulling her rolling suitcase behind her, she made her way out of the apartment toward her car. Roxi stood at the door and waved, before turning back inside. Moira was both excited and nervous about this next week. A whole week in New York with Cord. Would he be different than what she saw on St. Lucia? She shook her head at her foolishness.

'Bloody hell Moira, get your act together. Cord loves you and you love him. You know who he is and the city he lives in won't change that.' She told herself as she navigated from the city.

***

Cord

Cord sat on the stoop of his brownstone watching for Moira. Cord had woken early that morning and like a madman, started cleaning his home. Not that it needed much attention, since he had a housekeeper that came in once a week to clean. Sally had asked him why he hired someone, and Cord simply pointed out it made sense given the hours he worked. After a quick cleaning, he made a run to the store to stock up on food for the week. Now, for the last hour almost, he had been sitting outside keeping an eye out. He couldn't explain why he was nervous about having Moira here in his home, but he was. He looked up when he heard a car. He felt himself break into a smile as the blue civic pulled to stop in front of his home behind his truck. When Moira climbed out and rounded the hood, he stood and hurried toward her. He reached out, pulled her into his arms and kissed her. He felt Moira's arms wrap tightly around him as she returned his kiss. It felt like it had been forever since he had last held her, and she felt so damned good in his arms. Slowly they parted and Cord reached out to caress her cheek.

"Hi baby."

"Hi yourself."

"I've missed you Moira. So damned much."

"Aye, I've missed you too Cord."

Keeping her tucked into his side, they moved to her car where he pulled the suitcase from the backseat. Cord then steered them up the steps and into his home. He led her upstairs where she placed her suitcase at the foot of his California King. Cord didn't miss the longing that glittered through her eyes when she saw the bed. He felt his dick start to harden at the thought of having her spread out beneath him on the large bed. But that was for later.

"So, how about a tour first, then we can either go out and grab a bite before we start getting ready for the concert tonight. Or option two, you can grab a shower and I'll whip up some lunch and then you can catch a nap if you'd like." Cord suggested.

"Would you be too disappointed if I went with option two?" Moira asked nervously.

"Moira, I wouldn't be disappointed. I know you just spent nearly three and a half hours in the car. So, tour, shower for you, food, then a nap. We don't have to be at the bar until five, so we have plenty of time." Cord answered, kissing her forehead.

"Sounds like a plan boyo." Moira nodded.

***

Cord

Cord had just sat the plates on the table when he caught Moira stepping into the room. She was dressed in loose yoga pants; a tank top and her red hair was now a deep burnt red and swept up in a plastic clip atop her head. "You're just in time baby. I figured something light so went with grilled cheese sandwiches and kettle chips. And of course, sweet iced tea."

"That sounds perfect." She smiled.

Cord pulled out her chair for her and after she sat, he dropped a kiss to the side of her neck, making her giggle and shiver. He then moved and took his seat across form her. "How are your folks doing?"

"They're doing good. They told me to tell you and Collen hello and hopefully soon you two can get out to DC. I know da would love to take Collen to a Nationals game. Well, you and me too if we wanted." Moira replied.

"Collie would love that. While I have a favorite team, he just enjoys the sport for the game itself."

"And who is your team?" she quizzed, quirking an eyebrow.

"Uh-oh, why do I get the feeling this is some kind of test?" he retorted. When she simply cupped her chin waiting, he sighed and bit the bullet. "Fine. My team is...Atlanta."

Moira's eyes widened, "Well, I didna expect that. I figured you to be a Yankees or Mets fan."

"Your turn." He challenged.

"Oh, that's easy, Astros." She shrugged. "As you can imagine, last season things were heated between me, da and Sean. They are die-hard Nationals fans. Da was always fascinated with American baseball and fell in love with the Nationals. Course, Sean was a miniature version of da and well, there you go."

"Then how in the hell did you become an Astros fan?"

"Two words...Nolan Ryan."

Cord opened his mouth then closed it again. "Okay, you got me there."

Giggling, Moira reached for her glass. After a sip, she spoke again, "What are the plans for tonight? You said we had to be at the bar by five."

"That's right. Me and Collen will be there to make sure everything is set up for the band and whatnot. I was thinking we could grab a bite about four at this pizza place near the bar. We'll be at the Manhattan location which is maybe ten blocks from Times Square."

"Which pizza place?"

"Joe's."

"I love them. Me and Roxi's suite mates in college took us there our first night. I always get a large pizza to go when I headed home after meeting Holly and end up eating half of it on the drive." Moira grinned.

"Then Joe's it is. Figured we better have a full stomach tonight if we plan on drinking." Cord said.

"Hope your bar has good Irish whiskey boyo. And believe me, I'll know." Moira warned.

"I have the last name O'Brien; you think I'd be allowed to HAVE a bar if I didn't stock the good stuff?"

Moira burst out laughing and Cord soon followed. After they finished eating, Moira helped him wash the few dishes before they headed upstairs to grab a small nap. Stripping down to their skin, he set the alarm on his phone before climbing in first and pulled Moira into his arms, making her sigh in contentment. He loved how well she fit into his arms, hell into his life. In minutes he saw that she was sound asleep. Laying a gentle kiss against her lips and tucking her more securely in his arms, he followed her into sleep.

***

Moira

Moira sat at the bar and watched as Cord and Collen moved all around with the stage crew of the band making sure everything was ready to go. The concert would start at seven and the crowd would be let in starting at six. When she and Cord arrived at the bar an hour ago, already the line was forming. She figured that, by now, the line was halfway around the block with only twenty minutes before the doors opened.

"So, you're the one who has Mr. O'Brien walking on cloud nine lately." A female voice said, pulling Moira from her thoughts.

"Huh? Oh, I...I guess." Moira stuttered.

The woman was petite, her black and purple hair done in a pixie cut. The woman was beautiful, Moira couldn't deny that. She wore a black tank top that showed off both her arms which were sleeved in artistic tattoos. Her look was completed with black ripped jeans and boots. As Moira looked over the woman, she felt the woman looking over her as well. The woman then smiled.

"I'm Kat, the head bartender here." Kat stated, extending her hand.

"Moira Donovan." Moria smiled, shaking Kat's hand.

"The author?" Kat gaped. Moira nodded. "Wow! Do you think you could sign my book? I mean if it's not..."

"I'd love to." Moira beamed.

Kat spun on her heel and darted off. She returned a few moments later with a bag from Barnes & Noble. Kat withdrew the latest book Moira had out. Moira took the book and pen from Kat and instantly signed her book. "Oh, thank you. I started reading your stuff my last year of college. Course that was about four years ago. I have to say this, when Mr. O'Brien came back from his trip, he looked so happy. Collen told me that he met someone when I asked what brought on the change."

"I'm glad I make him happy." Moira said.

"You do Ms. Donovan."

"Please call me Moira."

"Moira then. Well, I gotta go get ready. Thanks again for the book. And one more thing, take care of Mr. O'Brien. He's a good man and deserves someone special." Kat added, before walking off.

Moira was stunned and touched. It seemed that Cord's employees cared about their boss and wanted him happy. Well, if fate was on her and Cord's side, she would do everything she could to make him happy. She turned and found Cord walking her direction. She met him halfway across the room and was instantly pulled into his strong arms and his lips finding hers, making her head all fuzzy.

"That was nice." She giggled.

"It was. I saw you talking to Kat." He said, leading her to a nearby bar stool.

"Aye, I was. At first, I thought she was going to be a problem." She nodded.

Cord started laughing, "Oh don't get me wrong, she can be a ball buster, but underneath it all she's a great girl. I met her right after she graduated college. Kat is a smart girl and has plans beyond being a bartender. She has a degree in business management. In fact, Collen and I are thinking of making her the new manager here."

Moira felt her eyes widen. "Really?"

"Yep. See, our current manager Larry is leaving next summer. He and his wife are moving to Albany to be closer to her dad. She's a nurse and her dad isn't doing good health wise. They are only waiting another year since their oldest is in eighth grade. They don't want to uproot him in the middle of the school year and figured starting over right before he starts high school was a better option." Cord explained.

"Makes sense. Starting over as a freshman at a new school anyway is a bit less shocking." Moira nodded.

"Anyway, Kat knows how this place runs. If she agrees, we'll have her and Larry start working together right away. That way the transition for her and the rest of the staff will be smooth."

"She seemed pretty protective of you."

Cord chuckled, "And me and Collen are protective of her. She's like a little sister for us. Was she rude?"

Moira smiled, "No, no. She just said since you came back you looked happier and that she was glad I made you happy."

Moira gave a squeak of surprise when Cord pulled her off her stool and onto his lap. Before she could speak, his lips found hers. Moira sighed and melted into his arms, giving in to his kiss. She felt lightheaded when he finally released her. Slowly, her eyes opened and met his. There was so much love and lust burning in his hazel eyes, it stole her breath and made her heart pound. She licked her lips but couldn't seem to speak.

"Moira, you do make me happy. The happiest I've been in...hell I can't remember when I've ever been this happy."

"Oh Cord. I could say the same. I'm so glad we met. I love you."

"And I love you too. Now, let's get ready for the party."

"Yes. I also promised Roxi I would try to get a picture and autograph of the band." Moira nodded, laughing.

"I think we can arrange that." Cord grinned.

CHAPTER SIXTEEN

Cord

Cord eased the bedroom door open and smiled. In the middle of his bed lay Moira. The thin sheet draped over her naked body, enticing him with memories of the night before. After a successful evening at the bar, he and Moira had returned home where she surprised him. Oh, he knew from St. Lucia that she was a hellcat, but last night had been an eye opener. The moment they walked into the house, Moira had spun and pinned him to the door before kissing the hell out of him. He had been so shocked and so turned on at the move.

She had then proceeded to give him the best blow job he ever had right there in the entryway of his house. After he exploded in her mouth, Moira stood and with a sexy smile started stripping while making her way toward the stairs. Cord had been helpless but to follow his Irish siren upstairs to the bedroom. Cord slowly shook his head to clear it and walked to the bed. He sat the two coffee mugs he held on his nightstand and slipped back into bed, pulling Moira toward him. She moaned a little but didn't fully awaken.

He leaned down and kissed her. Softly, slowly, coaxing her to respond to him. She didn't disappoint and her body shifted. He moaned feeling her beginning to hump his thigh. "That's its baby. Ride my thigh."

"Cord," Moira moaned, her voice still laced with sleep.

Cord felt his erection coming to life as he felt her grow wetter against him. Christ, he wanted her. He wanted her now. He shifted them so he was now over her. He watched as her eyes open just as he thrust slow and deep into her. Moira gasped his name, those blue eyes of her, those hypnotizing eyes widening. Cord took his time with her. No words were spoken between them, their eyes telling one another everything. When Cord finally came, it was in perfect sync with Moira. Their joint climax left them both trembling. Rolling onto his side, Cord tucked her against him, still buried deep inside her.

"Bloody hell Cord, that was...almost spiritual." Moira breathed.

"I agree." Cord sighed, peppering her neck with slow languid kisses.

"Mmm, that feels good."

"I'm about to make you feel good all over again Moira." Moira started to speak, but Cord just rolled his hips, her words dying in a long gasp. Cord rolled his hips again. "This is what you do to me woman. I can't get enough of you. Your body, your pussy."

"Yes Cord. I want..."

"Tell me baby. What do you want?"

"More. Please."

Cord couldn't deny her and rolled them over once more. Kneeling behind her, he gripped her hips and thrust again. Moira's cry of pleasure sounded like the sweetest music he had ever heard. Unlike the first round, Cord could no longer hold back. He slipped one arm around her, caging her against him, his arm banding her just under her breasts easing her up so they both were now kneeling. His thrusts became faster, harder.

"I can't hold back anymore...Moira...I..."

"Yes Cord. Take me. I want it. Now."

Obeying his woman, Cord let go and went wild. Moira was right there with him, matching his movements. As he thrust forward, she would rock back, taking him deeper. Her head was thrown back against his shoulder. He growled when she began speaking in Irish. Though he didn't understand the words, her actions told him she was demanding more. Demanding all of him. In moments, she screamed his name as her body locked up in an orgasm. He followed her, her name erupting from his lips as he poured himself into her.

"Holy hell," he gasped, as they fell against the mattress. "That was amazing."

"Aye it was," she panted.

Slowly he eased from her, both hissing as her vaginal muscles tightened, trying to keep him inside her. "Christ, I think I created a sex fiend."

"I think you did." She laughed.

"Let's grab a shower. Then we can sit naked in bed and enjoy our coffee." He said.

"Sounds like a plan." She agreed.

***

Moira

"So, I take it last night was a success?" Moira inquired as she and Cord walked down the sidewalk.

"I think it was." Cord answered. "Collen and Kat were still counting the drink profits when we left."

"It looked like the bar was hopping all night."

"Yes, I think my bartenders and waitstaff will be exhausted today."

Moira chuckled. She took in their surroundings. Cord's neighborhood was a quiet little place, which seemed surprising since it was New York. His home was in an older part of the Bronx, but the neighborhood was well maintained. He had told her that the people had fought tooth and nail to keep the troubles of the city out of their little pocket. When they turned into a park, she smiled as a group of teenagers waved and called out to Cord. It was obvious to her, then and there, that Cord was well known and liked by his neighbors.

"Hey Senor O'Brien." A boy of about sixteen greeted, walking up with a basketball tucked under his arm.

"Hey Rico." Cord smiled.

"Is this the Senorita you told us about?" Rico asked.

"It is. Rico, this is Moira Donovan. Moira, this Rico Arzola. He and his family live two houses down."

"It's nice to meet you Rico." Moira smiled, offering her hand.

"Senor O'Brien has talked about you a lot." Rico grinned.

The young man surprised her when instead of shaking her hand, he took it and kissed the back of her hand. "Awe, no eres el caballero?"

Rico's eyes widened at her calling him a gentleman in his native language. "You speak Spanish?"

Moira giggled, "Only a little. I live in DC and come to New York often to visit my editor and publisher. My editor Holly, lives in Spanish Harlem and she taught me a little. Course, with me being Irish, my Spanish isn't all that good."

"It's better than mine. Rico has been trying for a few years now to teach me and I still can only say 'hello' and 'my name is.'" Cord laughed.

"Well, my friends and I were wondering if you'd like to play a game of basketball?" Rico asked, looking up at Cord hopefully.

"Oh, um..."

"Cord go play. I'll sit right there on the bleachers and cheer you on." Moira insisted.

Cord kissed her cheek and followed Rico. Moira made her way to the bleachers and took a seat next to two women, one Hispanic or Puerto Rican and the other African American, both who looked to be in their early to mid-forties. The ladies studied her before one of them spoke up.

"Are you a friend of Senor O'Brien?"

"Aye. We met on vacation..." Moira began.

"Oh! You're the one Mr. O'Brien told our boys about. I'm Leticia Jackson. Those are my boys there, Travis and Aaron. This is Camilla Arzola. Her boy is Rico." Leticia introduced.

"It's nice to meet you. Rico was quite the gentleman. When I offered my hand, he didn't shake it, but kissed it." Moira replied.

Camilla smiled, "I try to teach him to be el caballero. Today, too many jóvenes have no respect."

"Ain't that the truth." Leticia agreed. "My sister lives in Harlem and her oldest boy got mixed up with some gang bangers last year and he's now in juvie. I told Aaron and Travis if I ever caught them doing that nonsense they wouldn't have to worry about the police. In fact, they'd be wanting the police to catch them before I did."

"It's sad to see so many kids being mixed up with that. My Da is a policeman in DC and my ma is a nurse. They see it too much. They made sure me, and my brother Sean were taught better." Moira added, sadness creeping into her voice.

"Mr. O'Brien told us you are a writer?" Leticia questioned.

"I am." Moira smiled.

"I've read a few of your books. I enjoyed them." Camilla said.

***

Cord

Cord helped Moira into her chair at the restaurant he had picked out for dinner. The day had been a great one. After three games of basketball with the kids, he and Moira had returned home for lunch. He had then grabbed a shower and they spent most of the afternoon on his couch watching TV. When he told her, they were going out to dinner in Manhattan, Moira had hurried upstairs to get ready.

"So, what did you think of Mrs. Jackson and Señora Arzola?"

"I liked them. They really seem to respect you."

Cord smiled a little. "I try to do what I can to help the kids. Growing up, I would always hear or see on the news the stories of kids falling into drugs and stuff. When I moved into the neighborhood and saw how close-knit it was, I promised I would help to keep it that way. In fact, one of Rico's cousins is my bartender at my Bronx location. He's a good kid, well, young man."

"You're a good man Cord O'Brien." Moria stated, taking his hand.

Cord squeezed her hand, then lifted it to his lips. They fell into a comfortable silence as the perused their menus. Yet Cord was unable to stop himself from sneaking glances at her. She had come downstairs in a beautiful purple halter dress that hugged her curves. Silver heeled sandals adorned her feet and that gorgeous mane of fiery hair was down and currently a section was draped over her shoulder. She looked beautiful. Of course, Cord thought she would look beautiful to him if she wore nothing but a burlap sack.

Their waiter appeared and quickly took their orders and menus. Cord reached for her hand and was about to speak, but he saw Moira stiffen and a soft gasp escaped her. Frowning, he shifted to look behind him where Moira was looking. He saw a couple a few feet away being led to their table. A moment later, Cord realized the man was looking at him and Moira. The man was dressed in an expensive looking tailored suit of navy blue. He looked to be Cord's age with sandy blonde hair slicked back. While the man dressed for success, Cord didn't like the look of him.

"Moira, who is that?" Cord asked.

"Th...that's Phillip." Moira stammered.

Cord turned when he sensed someone at their table. "Can we help you?"

Phillip ignored Cord's question and faced Moira. "My, my. Isn't this a coincidence."

"And you are?" Cord demanded, not liking the affect this guy's presence was having on Moira.

"I'm Phillip Clark. I'm the Public Relations Manager for the Mayor." Phillip introduced, making his voice sound important.

"What do you want Phillip?" Moira asked, seeming to come back to herself.

"I just wanted come over and say hello to an old friend Moira. Is that a crime?" Phillip replied.

"From what Moira's told me, you two aren't friends." Cord stated.

Phillip finally turned and fully faced Cord. Cord knew the man was sizing him up, like a butcher inspecting a cut of meat. "And you are?"

Cord rose to his full height. He towered over Phillip and took a small bit of pride when the man took half a step back. "Cord O'Brien."

Phillip's eyes lit up in recognition. "The owner of O'Brien's Tap?"

"That's right." Cord nodded. "Now, if you would kindly return to your dinner date and leave me and Moira alone, I would greatly appreciate it."

Phillip tugged at his suit jacket, as his eyes became glacial, "Well then, I come over to say hello to an old friend and I'm met with rudeness. Can't say I'm surprised though. Moira here never seemed to learn how to behave in polite company. Even in DC she never could mingle with those of importance properly."

Moira was on her feet, "How dare you. You were the one who took every opportunity to insult me when you lived in DC. Seems you're the one who doesn't know how to behave."

"I suggest you walk away Mr. Clark. Now." Cord hissed, moving to Moira's side.

Before Phillip could retort, a voice spoke up, "Well hello Mr. O'Brien."

Cord looked and saw the Mayor himself walk up behind Phillip. "Hello Mr. Mayor."

Phillip's eyes widened and he quickly spun to face his boss. "Mr. Mayor sir, I didn't know you were here."

"Obviously, Mr. Clark." The Mayor said, disdain tinting his voice. "I think perhaps you and your..." the Mayor turned to study the blond woman who had accompanied Phillip. She was currently checking her makeup in a handheld mirror. "Friend, find another establishment to eat at."

"But...but I had to wait six months for a reservation..." Phillip stuttered.

"Not my problem. You flaunt yourself over to Mr. O'Brien's table, proceed to insult him and his charming guest. I will not stand for any of my staff to conduct themselves in this way. Leave Clark, and first thing tomorrow morning I want you in my office. Is that clear?"

"Yes sir." Phillip answered meekly then rushed off.

"Thank you, Mr. Mayor." Moira said, embarrassment showing.

"Ms. Donovan, you have no need to apologize. I must apologize for the rudeness of my staff member. I hope this incident will not disturb your meal."

"Thank you, Hank." Cord said, offering his hand to the Mayor. "If you hadn't stepped in, I'm sure I would have punched him."

"I gathered, which is why I stepped in. I was at the table next to you and heard it all. I think Mr. Clark will find I am unforgiving on matters like this. Well, you two enjoy your meal. Good evening." Hank smiled and turned away.

***

Moira

Moria sat on the stoop and sighed. After dinner, they returned home and she quickly stripped out of her dress, threw on some yoga pants and a tank top before coming outside. She turned her head when she heard the door open and close. When Cord sat beside her, she just leaned against him as his arm eased around her shoulders. She was silent for a few moments then finally spoke.

"Why did he do that? Phillip, I mean?"

"Baby, I think he was trying to intimidate you. When you saw him, you looked shocked?"

Moira nodded. "I was Cord. I haven't seen him in a year. I had heard he was in New York, but never thought I would actually run into him."

Cord kissed the top of her head, "Moira, men like him, they're not worth your time. You are in a class of your own and he will never understand what a class act you are."

"I wasn't lying when I said he insulted me. The last six months we were together, he was always putting me down in public. He would play it off as a joke and the politicians we were around either believed it was a joke or didn't catch on. Not sure which. Finally, I had enough and left him." Moria explained.

"I wish I had hit him now." Cord growled.

"No." Moira said, turning and cupping his face. "You are better than him boyo. You hear me? You make me feel beautiful. Special. Loved. That's what's important now. You and me. Not that asshat. Okay?"

"Okay." Cord nodded, leaning in, and kissed her. "You are beautiful and special to me. And I love you."

"I love you too Cord. So very much." She sighed. "And thank you, for defending me tonight. It was nice knowing I have a man like that when I need one."

"My pleasure." He said.

CHAPTER SEVENTEEN

Cord

Cord shut down his computer with a sigh. Just as Al had predicted, the numbers of attendance and sales for O'Brien's Tap had indeed increased. After the success of the private concert back in June, things had only gotten better. It was now August and Cord and Collen had been busier than ever. Today Cord was taking a three-day vacation and driving out to DC to see Moira. Over the last two months they had seen very little of each other.

For Moira, she got the edits done on her new story and her publisher had pushed up the release date from September, to the last week of August. While Cord was happy for her, he knew that starting next week Moira would be tied up with book signings and such for nearly six months. Moira had already told him of several author events she was scheduled to attend from September until just before Christmas. Cord wanted to spend what time he could with her before all that started. Grabbing up his keys, he headed for the door and clicked off the light before walking out.

"You're heading out?" Kat asked as he stepped into the main room.

"Yeah. Collen will be around if you need anything." Cord nodded.

Kat leaned against the bar and grinned, "Off to see your girl huh?"

"I am. In about two weeks she's going to be busy with her new book tour and several author events she's got scheduled. Figured we'd try to get at least three days in before the craziness picks up." Cord chuckled.

"Well, tell Moira hi for me and that I can't wait to read the new book. You get out of here and you guys have fun." Kat said.

Cord gave her a wave and headed for the door. In less than an hour he had grabbed his bag from his house and was on his way toward DC. The further he got from New York, the more relaxed and excited he seemed to get. Yes, he loved what he did as did his brother, but with the upswing in business he seemed to be working longer hours than he had before. After this weekend, he would talk to Collen and see about moving forward on the project he had been considering since their mom had come out to visit.

***

Moira

Moira did a quick walk-through of her apartment. She had just got a text from Cord saying he had just hit town and would be there soon. Moira felt butterflies flapping in her stomach. This would be the first time that Cord had come to see her and for reasons she couldn't fathom, she was nervous. The last two months had been a whirlwind for them both. Cord's bars were seeing an influx of business and as for her career, she was seeing the same thing. Pushing those thoughts away, she walked back into her living room just as the bell rang. Moira hurried to the door, flung it open, and with a squeal leapt into Cord's arms.

"Now that's a hello." Cord laughed holding her tight.

"I've missed you boyo." Moira sighed; her arms locked around his neck.

"I've missed you too baby. Well, care to show me your place?" he asked.

Moira felt him lower her back to her feet. Taking his hand, she led him inside. Excitedly, she gave him the full tour of her two-bedroom apartment. Which compared to his brownstone, wasn't much, but she liked her place. It was just close enough to downtown for her to enjoy the city and just far enough away that the noise wasn't a bother if she wanted to sit out on her deck in the evenings.

"It's not much compared to your place, but it's mine." She grinned as they stepped onto the deck.

"It's a great place baby." He replied, sitting in one of the chairs and tugging her down onto his lap.

Moira sighed contently, feeling his arms encircle her. "I'm glad you're here Cord."

"Me too." He said, dropping a kiss against her neck. "So, any plans for tonight?"

"Actually, the only thing I have planned for today is to order enough Chinese for lunch and dinner, then we just stay in. Get reacquainted." She answered, hoping her eyes explained her meaning.

When she saw those gorgeous hazel eyes of his darken, she knew he caught what she meant. She giggled when he shifted his hold on her, stood, and walked back inside and straight for her bedroom. Cord walked into the bedroom, kicking the door closed and eased her down his body. Moira whimpered as she felt the hard planes of his body against hers. With her eyes on his, she reached between them and gripped his growing erection. Cord groaned.

"Seems someone else has missed me Cord."

"You're damned right he has."

With a slow stroke and squeeze, Moira released him and backed away. Smiling, she slowly began to strip for him. Her body grew hot at the look in his eyes. She moaned when the fabric of her demi-bra brushed against her nipples as she tugged it off. She couldn't explain it, but when Cord would look at her the way he was now, her whole body became one giant bundle of nerves.

***

Cord

Cord watched in apt fascination as his Irish beauty stripped for him. As each part of her body was unveiled to him, his dick throbbed. Those lush breasts, the swell of her hips, her delicious pussy. He wanted every inch of her. To touch her, tease her, taste her. Once she was completely naked for him, she backed up and climbed onto her bed. That was all the initiative he needed. Not taking his eyes from her, he stripped in record time.

"Christ woman, I just want to eat you alive." He growled, fisting himself.

"Oh Cord," she moaned, cupping her breasts.

"That's it, baby. Tease your body for me. I want to watch you and see you lose control for me."

Moira gasped as she started teasing her body for him. As she pinched and rolled her rosy nipples, Cord licked his lips. Her legs parted giving him a clear view of the bare v between her legs. God he couldn't wait to have her taste on his tongue again. Cord moved closer to the bed just as one of her hands slid down her body. He grinned when Moira gasped his name as her fingers quickly found her clit.

"Yes Moira, tease that clit. I want you wet for me. So wet that the second I lick that sweet pussy you explode."

"Cord...please..."

"I know what you want baby. You're almost ready for it."

Kneeling on the bed, Cord watched her closely. In the short time they had been together, he had become so in tune with her body he knew when she on the verge. The second her breath caught; Cord struck. His mouth covered her center and drank from her as she all but screamed his name. Her back bowed off the bed as he slid his tongue deep, wanting every drop of her pleasure. Looking up her body to watch her face, Cord moaned at what he saw. Her blue eyes were wide and locked on his, watching as he continued to eat her out. Their eyes still locked, he managed to wring another orgasm from her.

"Fuck you taste so good." He sighed, kissing up her body.

"I love your mouth on me." She gasped.

Cord gripped her hips, lifted them and in one thrust buried himself inside her. "Moira!"

"Cord..."

While Cord had wanted to take his time, now that he was balls deep inside her, that plan went out the window. Blanketing her body with his, he threaded their fingers together, lifting their joined hands over her head and started to move. Neither could speak as he thrust in and out of her. Yet their eyes said plenty. He could see when he hit that right spot, her eyes darkened, and her hips rocked more. Cord began moving faster and Moira matched his rhythm. Her blue eyes pleading for more of him. Harder. Deeper. He delivered and in moments both exploded.

****

Moira

Moira walked out of the kitchen and had to smile, "Well, don't you look pleased."

Cord glanced over from the sofa and patted his belly, "And why shouldn't I be? Good food, earth shattering sex, and my beautiful girl? What could be better?"

Moira laughed, handing him his beer, and curled up beside him. "Oh, um, me ma and da want you to come with me on Sunday for dinner. Seems Sean and his family are coming. Guess they want to meet you."

"And I want to meet them. Moira, if you're worried me and your brother will come to blows or something..."

"No, no. I love me brother and he may be a Marine, but I can still box his ears better than anyone and he knows that."

Cord chuckled, "Then what's wrong? When you told me, you looked sad almost?"

Moira sighed, "I guess I don't want to share you this weekend. In two weeks, I'll be booked solid till November and we won't see much of each other.

And from what you said, your bars are getting busier and busier. But when ma insists on something, you donna say no."

Cord hugged her close and kissed the top of her head, "I know what you mean there. My mom is the same way. Moira, we have the whole weekend together. If you just want us to stay right here in this apartment, ordering take-out, watching movies, and having sex then that's fine with me. If tomorrow you want to drag me to all your favorite places in DC, I'm up for that too."

Moira was floored. She grabbed his beer, sitting his and hers on the coffee table, she climbed into his lap, cupping his face, "Cord, do you mean it? If I wanted to be completely selfish and lock you and I here till Sunday dinner you wouldn't be mad?"

"Baby, I meant it. Whatever you want to do we'll do. I just wanted a weekend with you and don't care what we're doing. Of course, being a red-blooded man, I wouldn't turn down being locked here with you having sex all day and night." He teased.

Moira laughed and hugged him. "How did I get lucky to find you?" She pulled back and kissed him softly. "Okay, how about this? The rest of today and tonight we just veg out, clothes are optional," she winked, making him grin rakishly. "Tomorrow morning, I'll take you to my favorite breakfast place. Maybe we could take a walk around the rose gardens and then after that we'll just wing it. Sound good?"

"Sounds perfect Moira. Kind of sounds like our time in St. Lucia. Nothing concrete, just seeing what happens." He agreed.

"Aye. I'm not much of a planner outside of my writing." She smiled.

***

Cord

Hours later, Cord lay in Moira's bed feeling completely at peace. He glanced down and felt his lips curl up in a smile at what he saw. Moira was naked, curled up against him, her head on his chest sound asleep. All day they had snacked on Chinese, watched movies, and made love off and on. All naked. Well, they had stripped down after lunch anyway. He couldn't remember the last time he felt this relaxed and sated. Oh yes, he had been relaxed on St. Lucia, but here, in this moment it was different.

'Could it be because I'm head over heels in love with her?' he wondered.

Cord may have fallen in love with Moira on St. Lucia, but the longer they were together, he felt himself becoming more and more content with being near her. No woman had ever made him feel the way that Moira did. That made him more determined to move ahead with his secret project. He had crunched the numbers before and then Collen had told him about Al's findings and then the Five Finger Death-punch concert. When he returned to New York on Monday, he would reach out to Collen, Al and a few others and set up a meeting. It was time to reveal his idea to them.

Kissing Moira's forehead, he pulled her closer and started drifting off himself. If everything worked out as planned, by this time next year things would in place and the whole distance issue he and Moira currently faced would hopefully no longer be an issue. One way or another. Those were his last thoughts before sleep overcame him and he joined Moira in the land of sleep and dreams.

CHAPTER EIGHTEEN

Moira

Moira sighed as she stepped out of the shower. She was half-way though her book tour and yet another hotel. She thought she was in Austin, Texas, but wasn't one hundred percent sure. Ah, the joys of touring. Yet despite the exhaustion, Moira loved it. It gave her a chance to interact with her fans and sometimes other authors. Entering the bedroom, she headed for the closet to pick out what she would be wearing for the mixer tonight. She was here for not only her book, but also was participating in an author event. Tonight, was the mingle mixer, tomorrow she was speaking at a workshop in the morning and after lunch was doing a signing. She had just pulled on the flowing summer dress when her cell beeped. She reached over and plucked it up from the nightstand and couldn't stop the smile when she saw it was Cord.

"Hey boyo."

"Hey yourself beautiful. How's it going?"

"It's going. I'm fixing to head to a mingle mixer down in the ballroom."

"Sounds like fun." Cord laughed. *"How's the tour going? You knocking them dead?"*

Moira chuckled, sitting on the bed as she buckled up her heeled sandals, "I donna know about knockin' them dead, but it seems to be a success. At least that's what the publishing house keeps saying. I only have about another two weeks and then I get to go home."

"Well, how about instead of heading home, why don't you swing by New York. Maybe stay a day or two before heading back to D.C.? What do you say?"

"I say, you're on Cord. Should I call or just show up?"

"Tell you what, stop by the Manhattan location. I can give you the key to my place where you can grab a shower and relax for a bit. Okay?"

"Alright. I may have to do a bit of shopping then. I didn't pack any clothes for the weather in New York this time of year." Moira laughed.

"Then I'll take you shopping. Give me a chance to see what I'll be taking off you." Cord replied.

Moira had to bite back a moan at what his words promised. "Well, I must run or I'm gonna be late. I love you and I'll see you in two weeks."

"Love you too baby and can't wait to see you. Have fun."

Moira was still smiling when she hung up, slipped her phone into her clutch, and headed for the door. She made her way downstairs. When she entered the ballroom, the mixer was just getting started. Moira waved to a few authors she recognized as she moved through the crowd, looking around for the coordinator that her publishing house had sent along. After a few moments, Moira spotted Greg.

"Hey Greg." Moira greeted.

"Moira, there you are darling." Greg gushed, kissing her cheek. "I was wondering what was keeping you."

"Sorry, Cord called as I was getting ready." Moira replied.

Greg let out an appreciative sigh, "You are lucky. That man is a delicious specimen."

"Hey, hands off." Moira teased, causing them both to laugh.

The second Moira and Greg met; they had hit it off. He was sweet, funny, smart as a whip and an overall nice person. "Moira, if Cord even hinted that he was at least bi, you would have a fight on your hands, but seeing as the man is straighter than straight, you have nothing to worry about. Now, I came across a few people who I think you should meet."

***

Cord

Cord walked out of his office and toward the club area. The music was in full swing and from what he had seen on the security monitors, the place was packed. However, there was only one person he was interested in seeing tonight and that was Moira. He entered the bar area from a door to the right and quickly spotted Kat and Larry. Not long after the concert, Collen and Cord approached Kat about taking over for Larry. She was thrilled and accepted.

"Hey there boss." Larry greeted.

"Hey Larry, Kat." Cord nodded.

Kat grinned knowingly, "She's not here yet."

"That obvious huh?" Cord chuckled.

"If I see Moira, I'll either take her to you or flag you down. Why don't you go have a seat and I'll send one of the waitresses over with a drink?" Kat suggested.

Cord knew there was nothing more he could do but wait. Nodding to Kat and Larry he made his way through the crowd toward the owner's table that he and Collen kept at each of their locations. Taking a seat, he leaned back against the plush cushions and took in the scene before him. The table gave him a full view of the dance floor and bar. He had always loved to people watch and that's what he did now. Watched men hit on women, women hitting on men, couples flirting and dancing, friends out for a night of fun and drinks.

"Here you are sir." A soft voice broke through his thoughts.

"Thanks...Karina? Karina Lomax?"

"It's me." Karina grinned. "You seem to be doing pretty good for yourself these days."

"I guess. What are you doing here?"

"Uh, I'm working."

Cord chuckled, "I see that, but I meant in New York. Last time I saw you was at graduation and you couldn't wait to be rid of me and The Big Apple."

Karina sighed and perched a hip against the table, "Yeah. Cord, I'm sorry for that day. I was angry at myself and said a lot of things I didn't mean. You had this plan and seemed ready to take on the world. Me? I had a degree yes, but no job prospects. Out of our little group I felt like I was the only one of us with no plan, no future, nothing. I took it out on you and I'm sorry for that."

"Karina, you don't have to apologize for that. We're friends and sometimes friends hurt each other. It happens." Cord smiled, "So, other than working here, what brought you back?"

"I got a job offer as a personal assistant for a CPA firm on Wall Street. The pay is good, but out of tax season, things are a little slow, so I figured why not pick up a little extra cash. I work one night a week and every other weekend. At least, until tax season starts, then I'll see where I stand." She explained.

"That's great. I meant about the CPA firm. You always were good with numbers."

Cord wasn't sure what exactly happened next. One second, he and Karina were talking and laughing like old times and the next he found his arms full of Karina and her lips pressed against his. When he finally came to his senses, he gripped her upper arms and pushed her away and jumped to his feet. "What the hell were you doing?"

"That's what I'd like to know meself."

Cord spun and found a very pissed off Moira and an equally pissed off Kat.

***

Moira

"Moira!"

Moira turned and found Kat hurrying through the crowd toward her. Moira just laughed when the other lady gathered her in a bear hug. For such a petite woman, Kat had some strength in her arms. "Hey Kat."

"So, how was the tour? Cord said it looked like you killed it." Kat gushed.

"That's what the publishing house says too. I think it went well. I had fun but at the same time I'm glad it's over." Moira replied.

"I imagine. If you're looking for Cord, he's at the owner's table. Come on, I'll walk you over." Kat smiled.

Moira followed Kat through the crowd, the whole time just wanting to see Cord, hug him and kiss him. They hadn't physically seen each other since August when Cord had gone to DC for the weekend. That had been two months ago, and it was the longest they had been apart since meeting on St. Lucia. Suddenly, Moira bumped into Kat who was frozen like a statue. Moira looked around her and saw why. There was some busty brown-haired woman in an O'Brien's waitress uniform kissing Cord. What devastated Moira was the fact that Cord wasn't pushing her away.

She took several small breaths to stay calm. As she did, she saw Cord push the woman away and jump to his feet. "What the hell were you doing?"

Moira stepped closer, "That's what I'd like to know meself."

Cord spun facing her, "Moira..."

"You know what, just save it boyo." Moira hissed, walking towards the other woman, "And who the bloody hell are you?"

"I'm Karina Lomax. Cord and I dated back in college." Karina answered with a smirk, glancing from Moira to Kat.

Kat stepped up to Karina, "Ah, so you what, thought you would horn in on someone else's man? It's obvious you didn't mean that much to him if he pushed you away." Kat stated, watching Karina clench her fists and teeth. "Let me give you a bit of advice, you better walk out of here right now. And if you're REALLY smart you won't come back."

"You can't fire me..."

"Actually bitch, I'm the co-manager here and yes I can fire you. Now, get the hell out of here and you better hope Mr. O'Brien's lawyers don't press charges for sexual harassment against you." Kat growled.

Karina didn't budge. She simply crossed her arms and glared at Kat. Moira turned from the stare down and looked over at Cord. Taking several deep breaths, she finally found the courage to speak.

"Why?" Moira asked.

"Baby...I...I...don't know what happened. One second we were..." Cord began.

"You donna know? You donna know how you ended up kissing some tramp when you were supposed to be waiting for me?" Moira asked, surprised at how calm she sounded.

"I mean, I never even saw her move till she was kissing me..."

"Forget it. God, I was so stupid. I actually thought you were different." Moira said, a half laugh, half sob escaping her.

"No! Moira, please don't say that. I love you. I swear I didn't..."

Shaking her head, Moira began backing away from him. Not wanting to make a bigger fool of herself, she spun on her heel and rushed for the nearest exit. Behind her she could hear Cord and Kat calling for her, and Karina saying something, but she didn't stop. She had to get out of there and fast. About five minutes later, she had her bags from where she had left them at the coat check stand, and she was in a cab heading for Kennedy. At the airport, she booked the first flight to Reagan National, luckily it was in two hours. She felt hollow. Once again, she had let herself get played by a man. Well, never again.

From her purse, she heard the shrill of her cell. Pulling it out she saw it was Cord. She dismissed the call, turned the phone on silent and shoved it back in her purse. Maybe in a day or two she would talk to him and tell him it was over, but at the moment the numbness she felt since seeing that woman kissing Cord was turning into pain. A deep heart splitting pain and it took everything in her to keep the tears at bay.

When they finally called for her flight, Moira was relieved and quickly boarded the plane. She just wanted to get back to her apartment, maybe grab a hot scalding shower, and just curl up in her bed and cry. She wouldn't cry until she was in the cocoon of her home. At least that's what she told herself. Moira never felt or noticed the single tear that rolled from her eyes and down her cheek. It was the first of many that would fall over the next two days.

***

Cord

Cord sat in his office with his head buried in his hands. After Moira had run out, Karina had tried to comfort him, but Kat had stopped that and called security to escort her from the building. Cord had barely registered Karina warning him that she wasn't finished and that he'd be hearing from her lawyer. Cord didn't give a damn. All he cared about was Moira. He had called her nearly a dozen times, but she wasn't taking them.

"Cord?"

Cord looked up and saw Collen standing in the doorway with Kat. "I've lost her. She won't take my calls. I don't even know where she is."

Kat walked over and sat on the sofa beside him, "She's okay. I called the airports and she boarded a flight from Kennedy to Reagan about two hours ago."

"I also called her folks and her dad answered saying she had called them and that her mom was going to pick her up. I also explained what happened. Cord, there is more to this than you think." Collen added, his voice taking on a steely tone that told Cord his little brother was pissed.

"What are you talking about?" Cord questioned.

"After Karina was escorted out, I went to gather anything she might have had back in the lounge. I found dozens of pictures of you going back to just before you went to St. Lucia. I gathered them up and called the police. A Detective Schultz is on his way here now. I think she planned this." Kat answered.

Cord was now confused. "But why? I haven't seen or heard from Karina since we graduated college. She had broken up with me three days before the ceremony. Why would she do this?"

Before anyone could speak, there was a knock at the door. "Mr. O'Brien? I'm Detective Liam Schultz."

"Detective." Cord nodded.

"I understand there was an incident with a Ms. Lomax here tonight and she was escorted from the premises." Cord and Kat quickly filled him in on what happened and what Karina said as she was escorted away by security. Schultz sighed and rubbed the back of his neck. "Mr. O'Brien, your manager is right. Last night I got a call from Ms. Lomax's mother in Hoboken. It seems her daughter has been under treatment for bipolar disorder. Karina Lomax, checked herself out of the facility that her parents had sent her to for help back in April."

"Why would she come here?" Collen inquired.

"It seems that she had found out how successful you and your brother have become. I spoke to her doctors and the best they can guess is that it triggered her psychosis. Her mother said they had just received Karina's personal effects from the facility and there were dozens of internet articles about your bars and your success. Her parents had no idea where she was until two days ago when Karina told them that you and she were getting married." Schultz explained.

Cord was floored. "What? I didn't even know she was working here." He turned to Kat, "When was she hired and who hired her?"

"I don't know when. I was off last week. Remember, I had to go to take care of my mom." Kat said.

"Collen, go get Larry. Now! Only you, me, Larry and Kat can interview and hire people. I sure as hell didn't interview her." Cord ordered. He wanted answers and wanted them now.

***

Moira

Moira sat on the back porch of her parent's home. It had been a week since the disaster at Cord's bar. Her mom had picked her up at the airport and brought her to the house. When she and her mom walked in, her dad told her that Collen had called and told him what happened. Moira, however, wouldn't talk about it. She took her suitcases upstairs to her old room and didn't come out again until the next evening for dinner. For the last week, her parents had been trying to get her to talk about what happened, but she stubbornly refused. Then there were insistent calls from not just Cord, but Collen and Kat too. All the calls had gone to voicemails, but she could not bring herself to even listen to those.

"Okay, you need to get your shit together."

Moira looked up to see Roxi standing there, hands on her hips. "I don't want to talk about it Roxi."

"I don't give a damn. Your parents are worried about you and seeing you now so am I." Roxi stated as she sat in the chair next to her best friend. "Talk to me."

Moira could no longer hold it in. She told Roxi everything that happened that night. How she found Cord being kissed by some woman. "Roxi, he wasn't even stopping her. Not right away anyway. He couldn't even give me an answer as to why."

"Moira, did you give him a chance to explain?"

"So, this is my fault now?"

"No, no, that's not what I'm saying. Moira, you said yourself you turned and walked away, and that Cord was trying to get you to stop." Moira gasped as she realized Roxi was right. Roxi sighed and reached for Moira's hand. "Sweetie, you were tired, obviously hurting and in shock. Me personally I would have decked the bitch then him for good measure. There's no way you were thinking clearly."

"God, you're right." Moira groaned, burying her face in her hands. "Christ, what am I going to do? I'm not even sure if I want to know what happened. He, Collen and Kat have been calling all week."

"Did any of them leave voicemails?" Roxi demanded. Moira nodded. "Okay, give me your phone. Here's what we're gonna do."

***

Cord

Sighing, Cord hung up his phone. It had been a whole week since the Karina Lomax incident. In that week, a lot of stuff had been uncovered. Karina had been arrested the morning after she was escorted out of the bar trying to break into his house. Cord had gone to watch her interrogation and had been beyond floored at what he heard. Karina was telling Schultz that she and Cord were engaged. That she was pregnant with his child. After that, Cord had left the precinct. Cord consulted his lawyers and they agreed to press charges. In addition to being charged with attempted breaking and entering, Karina was also being charged with stalking and falsifying documents. All the information she had put on her application to get hired at O'Brien's Tap was false. There had never been a CPA firm.

"Any luck?" Collen asked, placing a cup of coffee in front of Cord.

"No. God Collen, I just want to tell her everything that's happening. I mean, I even left voicemails explaining, but I want to tell her face-to-face." Cord answered.

"Then why don't you get your ass in your truck and drive out there. She's still at her parents place right?" Collen said.

"I think so." Cord replied.

"Well, there you go. I'll pack you a bag. You go to her. Show her the police file and the stuff from the lawyers so she can see for herself that you're not lying. You don't come back here till you get her to listen to you and she sees everything. After that, the ball is in her court, but at least she will have all the facts." Collen explained.

"Yeah. Yeah, that's a good plan. Thanks Collie." Cord uttered.

"Go grab a shower and clean up. I'll get your bag handled and don't worry about the bars. You just focus on getting your girl back." Collen instructed.

Cord jumped from the sofa and rushed toward the bedroom. This was his last and only chance to get Moira back. He couldn't afford to screw this up. He quickly showered and shaved off the four days' worth of beard he had been sporting. He walked out of the bathroom, carefully picked out his clothes, dressed and headed downstairs for his home office. Methodically, he set about making copies of everything he had from the lawyers and police about what was going on with Karina, as well as the copy of the diagnosis from the facility in New Jersey that Karina had somehow managed to check herself out of.

An hour later, Cord was behind the wheel of his truck and making his way toward DC. He probably could have flown, but he would use the three hour or so drive to figure out how he would convince Moira to even listen to him. She wasn't taking his calls, so he wasn't even sure if she was bothering to listen to the voice mails as well. Well, he would just have to wing it as well, he supposed.

CHAPTER NINETEEN

Cord

Cord was almost to Moira's parent's house when his cell rang. He answered hoping it was Moira. "Hello?"

"Do you really want Moira back?"

Cord frowned, "Who is...Roxi?"

"You got it buddy, now answer my question."

"I want her back more than I need to breath."

"Good. Now, I want you to listen to me very closely and I'll help you get her back."

Cord listen to what Roxi told him. He pulled off into a gas station, typed in the location she told him to meet her, and in minutes was heading in the opposite direction. About ten minutes later, he parked outside a modern looking apartment complex. Grabbing the file of information on Karina, he climbed out of his truck and headed for the lobby doors. Following Roxi's instructions, he boarded the elevator and headed up to the fourth floor. He stepped off on Roxi's floor and found her waiting outside her apartment door.

"Roxi." Cord nodded.

"Cord." Roxi returned, then stepped aside for him to proceed her inside. She led him to the sofa, and both sat. "Okay, so let's get to the point. I talked to Collen about an hour before I called you and he told me you were coming here to talk to Moira. He also explained what had happened with that woman."

Cord handed over the file, "This is what I was coming to show Moira. After that everything would be up to her." Cord studied Roxi as she flipped through the files, watching her eyes widen more and more with each new piece of information. "You can imagine my reaction when all this stuff was revealed to me. I was shocked, confused, not to mention pissed off that she ruined things with Moira. Roxi, please. Please help me get her back. I need her."

Roxi took a slow breath as she closed the file. She looked up and studied Cord. She could see the heartbreak and pain on his face. The same look that had been on her best friend's face for the last week. "I'll help you Cord. Moira has been miserable since she came back. If you want to make this right, you're going to have to do exactly what I say. If Moira even knew I was helping you she'd have my head, probably yours, Collen's and her parents too."

"Wait, her parents?" Cord asked.

"Yes, her own parents. Maureen and Kiernan called me a few days ago and said that Moira barely leaves her room. Then yesterday, Kiernan said he called Collen. Look, you, and Moira belong together, and we all see that. Since she's not willing to come out of her funk on her own, we're going to help her." Roxi explained.

"Thank you. Roxi, I swear to you, I will not hurt Moira. In the short time I've known her, I know that she and I belong together and I'm willing to do anything and everything I can to prove that." Cord stated.

"Good. Now, let's get started." Roxi smiled.

***

Moira

Moira sat in the chair just staring out the window of her childhood bedroom. For the last week she only left the bedroom to shower and eat dinner with her parents. Yes, she knew her parents were worried about her, so was Roxi, but Moira couldn't bring herself to actually face the world. So, she just remained in her room. She watched as a blue jay landed on the branch of the oak tree outside the window. The bird just sat there staring at Moira. Moira just stared back. Almost as if she and the bird understood each other perfectly. Maybe on some level they did. After a few moments, the bird took flight and Moira wished she could do the same. Her thoughts were interrupted by a knock on her door.

"Moira? Honey, won't you come downstairs for lunch. Please." Maureen pleaded.

"No. I'll fix me something later." Moira answered, her voice sounding dull and lifeless, even to her.

Maureen sighed and stepped further into the room. Closing the door behind her, she moved to sit on the bed next to her daughter, "Moira, I understand you're feeling betrayed, but have you even bothered to listen to the voicemails from Cord?"

"Why? He betrayed me mum. What excuse could he bloody well offer to excuse it? Tell me?" Moira demanded.

"Honey, you told me and your Da that he tried to explain but you left before he could."

"I left before he could lie his way out." Moira hissed. She suddenly surged from her chair and started pacing. "God mum, how could I be so stupid? I honestly believed that he loved me. How pathetic."

"I donna think he was lying to you m'iníon ghrinn. Cord strikes me as an honest and loyal man. He's nothing like that bastard Phillip. It's because of him that you feel this betrayed by Cord. I believe, as does you Da, that there is more to this story. If you won't come down, at least listen to the voicemails. Cord may have explained things in them. At least then you would have some information." Maureen insisted.

Moira stopped pacing and faced her mom. Maureen said nothing more, only walked over, patted Moira's cheek and turned to leave the room. Once more engulfed in silence, Moira thought over what her mom had just said. Could she be right? Could Moira have overreacted? Taking a few slow breaths, Moira retrieved her phone from her desk and brought up the nearly fifty voicemails that Cord had left for her the past week. Scrolling down, she brought up the first one from that night. Hands trembling slightly, she opened it and listened.

***

Cord

"Well, what do you think?" Cord asked, facing Roxi, Kat and Collen.

"I still can't believe you pulled all this off in three days." Roxi gapped.

Kat snickered, "Oh he's been working on this little project for the last three months. He started it the day after Moira started on her book tour. He had been planning to tell her about it that night."

Roxi faced Cord, shock on her face. "Wow, you really do love her, don't you?"

"Yes. I've never loved anyone the way I love Moira and I'm damned well going to do everything in my power to prove it to her." Cord said. "The big question now is, can we get her here on Friday night?"

"Roxi and I will take care of that." Collen answered. "I've been talking to Kiernan and he's been fully informed about this little operation."

"Same with Maureen. They will make sure that Friday night Moira will be here. After that, the rest is up to you." Roxi added.

Cord let out a sigh of relief. This plan had to work. It was his one and only chance to get Moira back. He had to succeed. There was no room for error in this. If he failed, he knew he would simply fade from public life. Hell, as far as he was concerned, he had no life without Moira in his life. He needed that fiery Irishwoman at his side, in his arms and lastly in his damned bed. Plain and simple.

"Well boss?" Kat questioned, a knowing smirk gracing her lips.

"Then let's get this show started." Cord instructed.

***

Moira

"Excuse me?" Moira demanded in shock.

"You heard me Moira. Friday night, you will be going out with me and yer mum. We're going to dinner then to the grand opening of a new pub." Kiernan said.

"But Da..." Moira started to protest.

"No." Kiernan interrupted. He sighed and moved to her, cupping her chin as he used to when she was a little girl. "Is leor Moira, mo poppet. Enough is enough. You've been hiding in this house for almost two weeks. I know yer hurting, but you canna keep on hiding this way. Roxi went through a lot of trouble to get us the reservations at the restaurant and for the opening. And aye, she will be joining us for dinner and at the pub."

Moira bit her lip and nodded. Even as an adult she knew better than to argue with her Da. Moira turned and left the living room and made her way back upstairs to her bedroom. Yes, she knew her Da was right about her hiding from the world, but she still could not believe that he would force her to go out on the town as he was. But she knew there was nothing more she could do except to grin and bear it. Well, bear it anyway.

'Bloody hell, what am I gonna do?' she thought as she dropped onto the bed, burying her face in her hands.

Yes, she listened to the voice mails from Cord and while everything he said in them sounded plausible, she still couldn't bring herself to reach out to him and confirm them. The hard truth was she was still hurt by what she had witnessed that night and even hearing the explanations, didn't ease that hurt. Moira was stubborn and once she set her teeth in, it took time before she would let go.

***

Cord

Cord stood in the middle of the room turning in a small circle admiring all the hard work he and his team had pulled off. It was perfect. By this time tomorrow night, if things worked in his favor, he would have not only kicked off a new venue, but most importantly, he would have Moira Donovan back with him. *'Please, please let this work. I can't go on any longer without her.'*

"You ready brother?" Collen inquired, stepping up beside his brother.

"Collen, this will work right?" Cord asked, facing his little brother.

Collen placed his hand on Cord's shoulder, "Cord, everything will be just fine. By this time tomorrow you and Moira will be together again. I just know it."

"I hope you're right. God, Collen, I can't stand being away from her like this. I need her." Cord breathed.

"I know, I know. Just stick with the plan that Roxi came up with and it will all work out. Trust me." Collen smiled. "Now, come on. Let's get back to the hotel and get some sleep. I have a feeling we're gonna need it."

"Yeah. Let's go get some sleep." Cord agreed.

CHAPTER TWENTY

Moira

Moira and her parents walked into the restaurant. Moira still wasn't looking forward to the evening but knew that her parents and Roxi wouldn't let her out of it. They were immediately led back to the table where Roxi sat waiting. Moira watched as her parents hugged her best friend. When Roxi turned to face her, Moira just stood there. It was Roxi who moved first and gathered her into a tight sisterly hug.

"How are you holding up sweetie?" Roxi asked.

"I donna know honestly. I...I did listen to his voicemails, but..." Moira started.

"Moira, I know how you are and that you need time, but at least now you know what happened right?" Roxi replied.

"Aye, but that doesn't make it hurt less." Moira mumbled.

Roxi nodded in understanding as they sat down with Kiernan and Maureen. Internally, Roxi was happy with this new revelation. *'At least she listened to his voicemails. That should make the next phase a bit easier. Hopefully.'*

Moira sat at the table virtually silent as the conversation flowed easily between Roxi and her parents. Her mind however was toiling over what she was going to do about the situation with Cord. In his last message he had pleaded with her to call him. To talk to him, or at least call and just listen to what he had to say. All day she had to stop herself from doing just that. There was a big part of her that was afraid to hear his voice. Afraid that all the memories of their time together would overwhelm her and crush her. She missed Cord something fierce but her Irish pride was holding her back.

"So, tell us about this pub that we're going to." Kiernan said.

"All I know about it is that there isn't a place like it here in DC." Roxi began, "The owners built it to resemble an authentic Irish pub, inside and out. There will be food, drinks, and live music. I believe they plan to keep the musical acts strictly of the Irish nature for the time being, but I think in the future they may open it up a bit more depending on what the clientele wants."

"Sounds fun." Maureen smiled. "Heaven knows I've not been to a proper pub since me Da's wake nearly twenty-five years ago."

"Aye, I agree." Kiernan nodded.

"How did you find out about all this?" Moira questioned, before sipping her coffee.

"Oh, Jana told me. She was writing a piece on the pub for the paper and thought I'd be interested because of you guys." Roxi grinned.

"Because of us?" Moira inquired, arching a brow.

"Yes, you guys silly. Jana knows that your folks were born and raised in Ireland and that you guys are proud of your Irish heritage. It was her idea that I bring you all tonight. I couldn't think of a better way to bring you out of the hole that you call your bedroom than a night of good Irish whiskey." Roxi explained.

Moira hmphed, "Well, getting pissed on good whiskey sounds like a plan I guess."

***

Cord

Cord and Collen stood in the security room watching the monitors closely. Kiernan had texted him about twenty minutes ago saying they were on their way. Cord felt his heart pounding in his chest. Tonight, would be the first time in two weeks that he and Moira would be in such close proximity and frankly he was scared as hell at what she would do. Would she listen to him? Walk away? Clobber him with a whiskey bottle? All the above? So many questions and no inkling as to what the answers would be.

"You okay Cord?" Collen asked.

"I'm scared to tell ya the truth Collie." Cord sighed, reaching up to rub the back of his neck.

"Look, just be honest with her. Show her what you showed Roxi. After that, the rest is up to her." Collen said.

"And even if after all that she still doesn't want to be with me anymore?" Cord demanded, facing his little brother.

Collen didn't have an answer and that didn't ease Cord's fears one iota. He looked up and felt his heart skip. There, on the screen he watched Moira walk in with Roxi, Kiernan and Maureen. God she was as beautiful as ever. That gorgeous mane of red hair was down and some of it had fallen over her left shoulder. She wore an emerald green shirt that contrasted with her hair perfectly and hugged her torso deliciously. In the low lighting of the main floor, he could just make out the tight-fitting jeans she wore. His mind instantly drew up images of the last time he had felt her body against his. Cord called on his mental fortitude to keep the threatening erection at bay. He couldn't afford to blow this. If she took him back, there would plenty of time for that later. Tonight, he had to win her back first.

"She's here. John just walked them to their private table." Collen reported, clicking off his walkie.

"Okay. Okay, I can do this." Cord said.

"Yes, you can. Now get your ass down there and get your woman back." Collen pushed.

"Right." Cord nodded and headed for the door. There he paused and turned to face Collen. "Hey Collie, you might want to have an ambulance on call. Just in case she decided to clobber me."

"You got it." Collen laughed.

With a slow breath, Cord opened the security door and started to make his way downstairs. As he passed the main bar, he shared a look with Kat. She simply smiled and gave him a nod of encouragement. Cord navigated the sea of people dancing and having an overall good time as the Irish band he booked for the night played. The closer he got to the table, the more his heart pounded. Finally, he was there. Kiernan spotted him first and gave him a smile. When Moira turned, he watched the shock wash over her beautiful face.

"C...Cord?"

"Hello Moira." Cord said.

***

Moira

Moira was floored. Before her stood Cord. She couldn't stop herself from drinking in the man. He was as handsome as ever. He wore a soft looking cream-colored V-neck sweater that seemed to make his hazel green eyes glow in the low lighting. Her eyes traveled further down and saw he was in a pair of dark jeans that hugged his legs and thighs perfectly. Moira could feel her heart thudding against her ribs and her mouth go dry at the mere sight and closeness of him. She licked her lips, but when she opened her mouth nothing came out.

"Well, we'll leave you two to talk." Maureen stated as she, Kiernan and Roxi stood from the table.

It was then that Moira realized that tonight had been a set up and her parents and best friend had been in on it. As they passed her, Moira sent the three of them a glare and in turn they just smiled and walked away leaving her alone with Cord. She watched him closely as he sat across from her and placed a thick manila envelope on the table. Though Moira promised herself she wasn't going to speak first, she heard her voice break the silence.

"What are you doing here?" she demanded.

"Enjoying opening night of my new venture." Cord answered.

"What? You...you mean this place is yours and Collen's?"

"Yep." Cord nodded. "I got the idea after you and your parents had lunch with me, mom and Collen. While you were on your book tour, I started everything rolling. I got lucky with location and the rest just sort of fell into place."

She was shocked. Cord had done all this for her. "Cord..."

"Wait. Moira, let me talk first...actually, here." Cord pushed the envelope toward her. "I want you to look over this. I think it will explain a hell of a lot better than me trying to."

With a trembling hand, Moira took the envelope and opened it. Inside were dozens of papers, pictures, and such. As she flipped through them, she could feel her eyes widened at what she saw and read. Everything he had said in his voicemails had been true. Karina was an obsessively disturbed woman who had been stalking Cord for years. There were documents from doctors stating how delusional she was. How Karina had honestly believed that she and Cord were still a couple and were going to be married.

There were pictures from Karina's apartment and her various rooms from psychiatric hospitals that showed the home she believed she and Cord were going to have. A whole life she had built for the two of them. Moira couldn't believe it. This was the stuff you saw in movies, tv shows, or read in books. But she was holding proof that sometimes truth was in fact stranger than fiction.

"My god." She breathed.

"Moira, baby, I swear I never knew. The last time I saw her was the day of our college graduation. When I saw her at the bar that night, I was shocked. Then when she kissed me...I didn't know what the hell was going on. I found out two days later from her parents that she had found out about you and then everything sort of made sense about what she was doing that night." Cord explained. "She had been in New York, the weekend you came for the Five Finger Death Punch event and was actually at the bar that night and saw us together. Her parents figured that sent her on a downward spiral. Karina got herself hired at my Manhattan bar and planned her move. She must have heard me, Kat or Collen mention that you were on tour and so she just waited."

"I...I canna believe this." Moira said.

"I know, I couldn't either, but it's the truth." Cord replied.

Moira put everything back in the envelope, slid it back to him and finally met his eyes fully. "W...what happens now?"

***

Cord

"That's up to you baby. Moira, I love you and God knows I want you back. I'll do anything you want to achieve that. I also know how much this hurt you and shattered your trust in me. Phillip is the root of your reluctance to trust me now and Karina added to that fear. But you now know everything. The ball is in your court now Moira. It will be up to you what happens with us."

"Cord...I was so hurt and crushed when I saw you with her. I believed that you were just like Phillip, in that you didn't love me."

"No! Moira, I do love you. God, I love you so much. When you left that night, I felt like my whole world had been swallowed up by a black hole."

"I...I need time. I have to process all this Cord."

"I understand. Look, I was planning on tell you this that night. This pub, this was going to be my way of telling you that I want to be with you. I know your home is in DC and well, if that's your home it was mine too."

"What?"

"Moira, I'm moving to DC permanently. Collen will oversee New York and I will handle DC." Cord slowly stood from the table. "Moira, I'm not going anywhere. I'm not giving you up without a fight. I want you to know that. You take your time, process this. I'll be here when you've come to your decision."

Cord moved to her, leaned down and softly kissed her. He fought to keep his tears in check. He knew that while she could just as easily come back to him, she could, on the flip side, walk away from him for good. He pulled back, reached up to stroke her cheek, then turned and walked away. His very future now rested with his heart sitting at the table behind him. He only prayed that she would give him, give them, a second chance at a future. Together.

CHAPTER TWENTY-ONE

Moira

Moira stood on the porch of the home, trembling like a leaf. It had been three days since Cord had confronted her at his pub and told her, as well as showed her everything. After he walked away, she told her parents and Roxi she needed to leave and think. So that's what she had done. Moira had left the pub, gone to her parents' home, packed and returned to her own apartment. And for the last three days she thought about everything. Last night she made her choice and now she was here to tell Cord. Taking a deep breath, she knocked. Not a minute later, the door opened.

"Moira!"

"Hi Cord. Um, can I come in?"

Cord stepped aside and ushered her in. "Why are you here baby?"

Moira could hear the fear in his voice. He was afraid she was walking away for good. Well, she thought of the perfect way to give him his answer. Moira grabbed the front of his t-shirt, pulled him to her and raising on her tip toes, slanted her mouth over his. She felt his arms band around her as he returned her kiss. Moira's arms locked around his neck and she pulled herself up so she could lock her legs around his waist.

Cord being the smart man he was got the hint and turned on his heel. Moira had no idea where he was carrying her, but she didn't give a damn. All she wanted was to be reunited with him. She vaguely heard a door being kicked closed behind them moments before she was laid on a bed. When Cord pulled back, Moira reached for the hem of his shirt and yanked it up. It flew across the room seconds later.

"Moira..."

"I need you Cord. Now."

"Yes ma'am." He smiled.

In less than five minutes they were naked and tangled in each other on his bed. Moira sighed as her hands and mouth started exploring his body again. It had been so long, but she hadn't forgotten his body. She still remembered what turned him on, what made him wild. That's what she wanted. She didn't want sweet. Hell no, she wanted that fiery passion that brought them together in St. Lucia.

"Moira. God woman." He groaned as she took him in her mouth, his fingers tangling in her hair.

Moira moaned. She was taking no prisoners and when her eyes looked up, she saw that Cord's eyes were burning with need. Need for her. Need for them. Keeping her eyes locked on his, she watched him as he watched her take him. Taking what was hers. In mere moments Cord bucked, calling her name, and flooding her mouth. She had never seen anything so hot as seeing Cord come apart for her. Mewing like a kitten, Moira slowly cleaned him before kissing her way back up his body. When their lips met, she was flipped onto her back, Cord over her.

*****

Cord

"Now it's my turn Moira." Cord said.

"Aye Cord." Moira breathed.

Cord watched her as he began his own warfare on her. God she was trembling, and he loved it. When he saw her on his porch, he was afraid she was there to say goodbye. Those fears died a quick death when she kissed him. In her kiss she told him all he needed to know. She was his and he was hers. Down he moved. His hands, mouth, tongue moving over her skin. Making her moan and buck. Yet their eyes remained locked. Like her, he wanted, needed her to watch as he reclaimed her. His hands cupped her breasts as his mouth covered her. Moira cried his name.

She tasted as delicious now as ever. He was greedy and from how she moved against his mouth, Moira loved it. He watched her eyes close and she surrendered to him and it shot right to his dick. Her full submission. Her love for him. Everything about her turned him on. Thrusting his tongue faster Cord watched his world explode for him. Swallowing her release, Cord felt his erection spring to life once more.

"So beautiful Moira. I need you. Now."

"Yes Cord. Please."

That was all he needed. Her Irish lilt laced with lust. Rising over her still trembling body, Cord thrust into her. Moira's arms and legs snaked around him, trapping him to her. Cord captured her lips as they began moving as one. No words were needed now. Their bodies were saying it all. He wasn't being gentle, but that's not what they wanted. Gripping her wrists, he pinned them over her head as he drove into her. Their eyes locked. Blue and hazel green. Unspoken words passing between them as their bodies repeated them. Cord felt his release building fast and knew she was right there with him. When she started to scream his name as her orgasm hit, he kissed her hard and let go of his own.

***

Moira

Moira awoke with a sigh of contentment. She giggled when an arm tightened around her. "Mm, hi."

Cord dropped a soft kiss on her shoulder, "Hi."

She rolled in his arms, so she was now facing him, "I love you Cord."

"I love you Moira Donovan. These last few weeks were hell for me baby. When I saw you on my porch, I thought you were leaving me. Then you kissed me."

"Aye, I figured showin' you would be better."

"Yes. Moira, I'm sorry I hurt you. I will make it up to you however..."

Moira placed her finger to his lips, "No Cord, I'm the one who's sorry. I should have believed you. Should have known that you would never do to me what Phillip did."

"Move in with me."

Moira was floored. "W...what?"

"You heard me. I love you Moira. I want you with me always. We can start with you moving in here with me."

Moira smiled brightly at him. "Yes. Yes, Cord O'Brien, I'll move in with you."

Cord returned her smile and kissed her. Moira moaned as he shifted them, so he was fully over her. She arched her back when he eased himself into her. Slowly. Letting her feel every inch of his need for her. He reached down and moved her legs, so they now rested high on his hips. She felt her eyes flutter open and what she saw melted her heart. Cord looking down at her, his eyes full of love.

"Cord…shouldn't we…be making plans?" Moira gasped when he tilted his hips, sinking deeper.

"Later. We have all the time in the world now." Cord groaned.

"Aye. We do."

***

Cord

Cord carried the box up the stairs and into the bedroom. Now, his whole house it seemed was full of boxes and packing crates, but he still couldn't stop smiling. Moira was now officially living with him. In fact, he was carrying the last of her things. A week ago, he had asked her to move in with him and she said yes. That night, they had gone out with her parents and told them. Kiernan and Maureen had been thrilled for them and offered to help move Moira in. Even her brother Sean had helped. Things were now just as they should be. He had Moira back, the pub in DC was thriving and Collen said the bars in New York were doing better than ever.

"You're smiling." Moira said as she exited the master bath with an empty box.

"Yes, and I have a damned good reason to smile." Cord replied. He sat the box down and pulled Moira into his arms, kissing her slow and languidly. He felt her melt against him as he maneuvered them toward the bed. He eased her back and lifted his head. "I love you Moira Donovan."

"I love you too Cord O'Brien."

Don't miss out!

Visit the website below and you can sign up to receive emails whenever Michelle Kee publishes a new book. There's no charge and no obligation.

https://books2read.com/r/B-A-EDOD-QMDOC

BOOKS 2 READ

Connecting independent readers to independent writers.

Also by Michelle Kee

Blackout Security Inc.
The Soul of Archer

Standalone
St. Lucia Escapades

Watch for more at https://www.michellekeeauthor.com.

About the Author

Michelle Kee is a mother of two daughters and the wife of a Marine. For six years, she lived the life of a combat Marine wife and did so with pride.

She enjoys an eclectic range of music and often draws inspiration from it. When she's not plotting or writing, she can often be found reading or crocheting.

Originally from Houston, Texas, Michelle and her family now live in a small town in Ohio

Read more at https://www.michellekeeauthor.com.

www.ingramcontent.com/pod-product-compliance
Lightning Source LLC
Chambersburg PA
CBHW050521160726
48003CB00001B/407